John Paterson Smyth

The Old Documents and the New Bible

an easy lesson for the people in Biblical criticism - the Old Testament

John Paterson Smyth

The Old Documents and the New Bible
an easy lesson for the people in Biblical criticism - the Old Testament

ISBN/EAN: 9783337390471

Printed in Europe, USA, Canada, Australia, Japan

Cover: Foto ©Andreas Hilbeck / pixelio.de

More available books at **www.hansebooks.com**

The Old Documents

AND

The New Bible.

AN EASY LESSON FOR THE PEOPLE IN
BIBLICAL CRITICISM.

BY

J. PATERSON SMYTH, LL.B., B.D.,

Senior Moderator and Gold Medalist, Primate's Hebrew Prizeman, &c. &c.
Trinity College, Dublin.
AUTHOR OF "HOW WE GOT OUR BIBLE."

THE OLD TESTAMENT.

THIRD EDITION.

PREFACE.

In our grandfathers' days, in the simple loving
reverence with which the Bible was regarded it almost
seemed to men as if, clasped and covered complete, it
had dropped down from Heaven like the image of the
goddess Diana. It was much too sacred a thing to
be the subject of critical inquiry; to admit the possibility of mistakes in its text would have been little
short of heresy; while as for making an investigation
into the composition and genuineness of its books—
why, a man would as soon have thought of "botanising
upon his mother's grave!"

But "old times have changed." In this age of criticism nothing is too sacred to be questioned and investigated, and the present generation is accustomed to
see the most vital questions connected with the Bible
discussed with the utmost freedom.

Nor is the discussion confined, as in former days,
to the circle of scholars and theologians. The sounds
of attack and defence have reached the ears of "the

people " outside that circle, and excited a spirit of inquiry which, unsatisfied, may easily pass into one of doubt and uneasiness,[1] but which, rightly directed, cannot fail to lead to a more intelligent belief in the Bible and its claims. People want to be told without reservation all that can be told them about this Bible of theirs ; on what foundation it rests ; why they should believe in its genuineness, its authenticity, its inspiration, its correctness of transmission through all the centuries. Never before perhaps was there as much of unsatisfied popular questionings (often un-spoken questionings) about these matters as at the present day.

This book is one of a projected series in answer to these popular questionings. It covers only one part of the ground. It is not a book of " Evidences " in favour of the Bible but an attempt at an *impartial* history of facts. It is not an erudite treatise for scholars and students, but a simple effort to " shift knowledge into a more convenient position " for plain

---

[1] A striking confirmation of this comes to me even as I write. Before me lies an account of the Triennial Convention of the American Church, held last month, where one Report states of so simple a matter as the publication of the Revised Bible, *"not all the assaults of scep-ticism have so shaken the ancient reverence for the Scriptures in the minds of Christians at large!"* What an amount of ignorance about the Bible must be in the "minds of Christians at large " if that report be correct!   Could we have a stronger proof of the need there is of telling people all that can be told them about their Bible?

people who have little opportunity of studying such subjects for themselves.

Therefore I have tried to write it as simply as I could. I have aimed at clearness rather than at completeness. Therefore, too, I have as far as possible avoided cumbering its pages with references to learned authorities which would be quite out of the reach of such readers as I have in view.

It may be well to state here the plan of the book which is fully explained later on. It consists of three parts. The first deals with the Old Hebrew Documents and the question of their correctness; the second tells of other old documents and their use in testing and correcting the Hebrew; while the third part is a series of easy illustrations to show how this testing and correcting is done.

I have to thank Professor Westwood of Oxford for his kind permission to photograph three of the following plates from his *Palæographia Sacra Pictoria.*

J. P. S.

CHRIST CHURCH VICARAGE, KINGSTOWN,
February 1890.

LIST OF PLATES.

CONTENTS.

𝔅𝔬𝔬𝔨 𝔈.

THE OLD HEBREW DOCUMENTS

AND THE QUESTION OF

BIBLICAL CRITICISM.

CHAPTER I.

HEBREW WRITING, EARLIER AND LATER.

CHAPTER II.

SOME PECULIARITIES OF HEBREW WRITING.

CHAPTER III.

WHAT IS BIBLICAL CRITICISM?

CHAPTER IV.

A VIEW OF THE OLD MANUSCRIPTS.

CHAPTER V.

THE STORY OF THE MANUSCRIPTS.

THE EARLY AGES.

CHAPTER VI.

THE STORY OF THE MANUSCRIPTS.

THE MEN OF THE GREAT SYNAGOGUE.

CHAPTER VII.

THE STORY OF THE MANUSCRIPTS.

THE TALMUD PERIOD.

CHAPTER VIII.

THE STORY OF THE MANUSCRIPTS.

THE DAYS OF THE MASSORETES.

CHAPTER IX.

CONTENTS.

Book II.

THE OTHER OLD DOCUMENTS,

AND THEIR USE IN

BIBLICAL CRITICISM.

DOCUMENTS No. IV.

A BUNDLE OF GREEK BIBLES.

DOCUMENT No. V.

THE SYRIAC BIBLE.

DOCUMENT No. VI.

THE "VULGATE" OF ST. JEROME.

BOOK III.

THE NEW BIBLE.

A SPECIMEN OF

BIBLICAL CRITICISM.

CHAPTER I.

CRITICS AT WORK.

CHAPTER II.

SPECIMENS OF CRITICAL WORK.

CHAPTER III.

A FURTHER USE OF THE ANCIENT BIBLES.

Book I.

THE OLD HEBREW DOCUMENTS,

AND THE QUESTION OF

BIBLICAL CRITICISM.

GEN. i. 1–10.

בראשית א

בְּרֵאשִׁית בָּרָא אֱלֹהִים אֵת הַשָּׁמַיִם וְאֵת הָאָרֶץ׃

‏2 וְהָאָרֶץ הָיְתָה תֹהוּ וָבֹהוּ וְחֹשֶׁךְ עַל־פְּנֵי תְהוֹם וְרוּחַ אֱלֹהִים מְרַחֶפֶת עַל־פְּנֵי הַמָּיִם׃ ‏3 וַיֹּאמֶר אֱלֹהִים יְהִי אוֹר וַיְהִי־אוֹר׃ ‏4 וַיַּרְא אֱלֹהִים אֶת־הָאוֹר כִּי־טוֹב וַיַּבְדֵּל אֱלֹהִים בֵּין הָאוֹר וּבֵין הַחֹשֶׁךְ׃ ‏5 וַיִּקְרָא אֱלֹהִים ׀ לָאוֹר יוֹם וְלַחֹשֶׁךְ קָרָא לָיְלָה וַיְהִי־עֶרֶב וַיְהִי־בֹקֶר יוֹם אֶחָד׃ פ

‏6 וַיֹּאמֶר אֱלֹהִים יְהִי רָקִיעַ בְּתוֹךְ הַמָּיִם וִיהִי מַבְדִּיל בֵּין מַיִם לָמָיִם׃ ‏7 וַיַּעַשׂ אֱלֹהִים אֶת־הָרָקִיעַ וַיַּבְדֵּל בֵּין הַמַּיִם אֲשֶׁר מִתַּחַת לָרָקִיעַ וּבֵין הַמַּיִם אֲשֶׁר מֵעַל לָרָקִיעַ וַיְהִי־כֵן׃ ‏8 וַיִּקְרָא אֱלֹהִים לָרָקִיעַ שָׁמָיִם וַיְהִי־עֶרֶב וַיְהִי־בֹקֶר יוֹם שֵׁנִי׃ פ ‏9 וַיֹּאמֶר אֱלֹהִים יִקָּווּ הַמַּיִם מִתַּחַת הַשָּׁמַיִם אֶל־מָקוֹם אֶחָד וְתֵרָאֶה הַיַּבָּשָׁה וַיְהִי־כֵן׃ ‏10 וַיִּקְרָא אֱלֹהִים ׀ לַיַּבָּשָׁה אֶרֶץ וּלְמִקְוֵה הַמַּיִם קָרָא יַמִּים וַיַּרְא אֱלֹהִים כִּי־טוֹב׃

CHAPTER I.

I.

Hebrew Writing.

The reader is probably aware that the Old Testament, with some little exception,[1] is written in Hebrew, the "holy tongue" of the Jews. It is a branch of the great Semitic family of languages, so called because the nations to which they belonged were considered to be chiefly the descendants of Shem (Gen. x. 21). The Syriac and Arabic represent other branches of the same great family, and the increasing knowledge of them in recent times has thrown a good deal of light upon the language of the Old Testament.

On the opposite page we give a specimen from the first chapter of Genesis as it appears in an ordinary printed Hebrew Bible. Here is the first verse with its corresponding English—

בְּרֵאשִׁית בָּרָא אֱלֹהִים אֵת הַשָּׁמַיִם וְאֵת הָאָרֶץ:

In the beginning created God the heavens the and the earth.

From this it will be seen that the language is

---

[1] Portions of the Books of Ezra and Daniel, which are in Aramaic, the common dialect of Palestine after the Captivity.

A

written *backward*, as we should say, *i.e.*, from right to left. The pages are taken in the same order, the right hand before the left; and therefore, in the reading of a Hebrew Bible (if it be not too Irish an expression to use), the beginning of the book is always at the end!

II.

The Ancient Characters.

Now this specimen of our present Hebrew Bible belongs to the *later* or Assyrian writing. The characters differ from those in which the books were originally written, much as the clear Roman type of our present Bible differs from the old black letter of Wycliff's and Tyndale's versions. The ancient Hebrew or Phœnician writing does not exist in any manuscript that has come down to us, though it is rather like the writing of the Samaritan Pentateuch, of which we shall hear farther on. We have some old coins of the time of Judas Maccabeus which present specimens of it. There is also the famous Moabite Stone, discovered some twenty years since, the actual old slab on which Mesha "the sheepmaster," king of Moab, 3000 years ago had inscribed in these ancient characters his own version of the fighting with Israel.[1] In the frontispiece is a photograph of this ancient inscription, probably the very form in which the finger of God traced the words long ago on the two tables of

---

[1] See 2 Kings i. 1, iii. 4 ; 2 Chron. xx., &c.

stone on Mount Sinai. A cast of it may be seen in any good library.

And very recently, in a curious way, a new specimen has come to light. One day, in the summer of 1880, a number of boys were playing about the Pool of Siloam near Jerusalem. There is at the upper end a tunnel cut out of the solid rock, by means of which the Pool is fed; and one of the boys, while wading here, slipped and fell forward into the waters of the tunnel. It was a fortunate fall for us, if not for the boy; for, as he was recovering himself, his eye was caught by some marks like letters on a smooth part of the rock; and on a fuller investigation afterwards by competent scholars, this was found to be an inscription by the workmen of the tunnel, written in ancient Hebrew characters somewhere about the year 700 B.C.[1]

III.

The Shapira Manuscripts.

A few years later, and it seemed as if even the fame of these discoveries was to be entirely eclipsed. In the August of 1883, an immense sensation was caused in the learned world by the announcement of a most wonderful "find" of ancient Hebrew manuscripts in Palestine,—"the great climax," it was called, "of Biblical discovery."

[1] An interesting account of this inscription is given in the Bishop of Ossory's "Echoes of Bible History," where it is shown that the tunnel was most probably that made by Hezekiah, when he "stopped the upper watercourse of Gihon and brought it straight down to the City of David." See 2 Chron. xxxii. 2-4, xxxii. 30.

It consisted of fifteen leather slips, black with age as it would seem, and impregnated with the faint odour of funereal spices. They presented to the casual observer only the appearance of a plain oily surface, but on touching them with a brush dipped in spirits of wine, the strange old writing became visible,—forty columns of Deuteronomy in the ancient Hebrew characters, just like those on the Moabite Stone, and apparently dating from about the eighth or ninth century before Christ.

These precious documents were brought to the British Museum by a Mr. Shapira, a dealer in old manuscripts, who had already procured through the Arabs many literary curiosities, and he estimated the value of this new-found treasure at one million pounds sterling! A council of the greatest experts in the kingdom assembled to investigate the matter, and Biblical scholars almost held their breath awaiting the momentous decision, the importance of which was vastly augmented by recent controversies as to the date, composition, and authorship of the Pentateuch.

.   .   .   .   .

On Tuesday, August 21st, the decision was announced in a leading paragraph of the *Times.* The particulars of the investigation are extremely interesting, but the result only concerns us here. The Shapira bubble had burst! The much-talked of manuscript of the days of Jehoshaphat was found to have been written in the days of Victoria, one of the cleverest literary swindles perhaps ever recorded.

Thus ended the Shapira "discovery." Since that time nobody ventures to speak of the possibility of manuscripts yet existing in the ancient Hebrew writing.

IV.

The Handwriting of the Exiles.

When did the change from these ancient characters to the present square writing take place? That, reader, is not an easy question to answer. The Jews, of course, say in the days of Ezra. But the Jews have a trick of putting down to Ezra or to Moses every important event in the history of their Bible, so that this statement does not count for much. Probably the change was a gradual one, and began at or soon after the time of Ezra. The name of the new writing (Assyrian) would suggest that the Israelites brought it with them on their return from the exile, though, on the other hand, a tradition that they did so may have given rise to the name. But in any case, there is little doubt that it was in full possession in the days of our Lord. An interesting confirmation of this is His expression that even "one Yod or one tittle should in no wise pass from the law" (Matt. v. 18), implying that the Yod (the letter ‎ י) was the very smallest letter, as it is in the present writing, whereas in the old alphabet it was one of the largest.

The Samaritans still retain the ancient form of

writing, or rather a modification of it, and have always been inclined to plume themselves considerably on that fact. But the Jews do not care to be thus easily set down, and so the Babylonian Talmud cleverly turns the tables. " The law," it says, " was given to Israel in the holy tongue and in the ancient Hebrew writing. And it was given to them again in Ezra's days in the square Assyrian writing. The Israelites chose to themselves the holy tongue in the square writing, and left the old Hebrew writing to ignorant persons. But who are these idiots or ignorant persons? Rabbi Chasda informs us—the Samaritans ! "

CHAPTER II.

I.

Consonant-Writing.

There are some peculiarities about the Hebrew language which it is important the reader should know, that he may the better understand some of the questions which are the subject of Old Testament Biblical criticism.

The first is this, that *the Hebrew alphabet, both in its ancient and in its present form, consists of consonants only.* In the specimen given already, the little dots and marks underneath the letters represent the vowel sounds. But these marks are of comparatively modern date, certainly not older than about 500 or 600 A.D. In olden times the reader had only the consonants before him, and had therefore to supply the right vowel sounds himself in reading.

It is easy to see how in such a case the same word might be differently read according to the different vowels supplied. For example, in English, B R N might be read B$_a$RN, B$_o$RN, B$_u$RN, BR$_i$N$_y$, B$_a$R$_o$N$_y$, &c.; and if there were no vowel marks to indicate the sound, we should have to be taught, like the Jews, which word the writer intended.

II.
Curious Mistakes.

We have many instances of this inconvenience after Hebrew had ceased to be a commonly spoken language. The great Greek version of the Old Testament, the Septuagint, of which we shall hear later on,[1] is a case in point. It is full of discrepancies arising from this cause. Here, for example, are two Hebrew words in Deuteronomy, B z R and P s G H, which in our Hebrew Bible read Bezer and Pisgah, but which the Septuagint translators render Bozor and Pasgah. St. Jerome (A.D. 400), commenting on Gen. xv. 11, says that his copy of the Septuagint, by supplying the wrong vowels, tells that Abram, instead of "driving the fowls away," as our Bible has it ($V_a Y_a SH_{ee} B \, {}_o T_a M$), actually "sat down with them" ($V_a Y_{ee} SH_e B \, {}_i T_a M$)!

Or would the reader like a more sensational example, though we scarcely care to vouch for its truth. Here is a story[2] in the Jewish Talmud, in a comment on 1 Kings xi. 15, 16, where "Joab had smitten every male in Edom."

When he returned from the slaughter into the

---

[1] It is important that the reader should here impress this name on his memory, that it may convey a clear idea when he meets it again. For this purpose it might be well to glance forward for a moment to its story in Book II. p. 148.

[2] The story is told by Elias Levita in his "Massoreth Hammassoreth," p. 128.

presence of King David, "Why hast thou smitten them all?" asked the king.

"Because," replied the warrior, "so it is written, Thou shalt destroy every male" (Z_aK_aR).

"Z K R!" exclaimed the king, "we read it Z_eK_eR, every memory, every memorial of them."

Joab was enraged. He went immediately to his Rabbi, and angrily demanded, "How teachest thou to read this word?"

"Z_eK_eR, memory," replied the Rabbi.

Joab drew his sword.

"Why?" asked the terrified teacher.

"Because it is written, 'Cursed be he that doeth the work of the Lord deceitfully'" (Jer. xlviii. 10).

The Rabbi does not seem to have been at all surprised at this feat of quoting from a prophet who was not born for many years after. He tried to argue his case, but all in vain. Joab was nothing if not scriptural. His quotations were as ready as those of Cromwell's Ironsides, and about as soothing too. "It is written also," he thundered, as he drew his flashing blade again, "Cursed is he that keepeth back his sword from blood!"

For the reader's comfort be it recorded that the historian leaves it an open question whether the unfortunate tutor was let off, or whether his zealous pupil, by depriving him of his head, cured him for ever of false pronunciation. The story, in any case, will illustrate our point as to the possibility of error in Hebrew when written without vowels.

III.

How to Read without Vowels.

To the English reader this consonant-writing would seem a very great danger to the purity of the Hebrew Scriptures, but the danger was really a very slight one after all. In the first place, Eastern nations depended on the memory much more than on writings. The Jewish scribes could repeat whole books of their Scriptures with perfect ease, just as the Mohammedans repeat their Koran to-day. And thus the true reading of the vowelless words was handed down from one generation to another. When a young Jewish pupil began to read the Scriptures, the page of consonant words was opened before him ; the scribe, his teacher, read over the words, and he repeated them after him, with their right pronunciation. His task, perhaps, might be expressed as a saying by heart with the help of the consonants. We Westerns have but little notion of the ' extraordinary powers in this respect possessed by the Eastern mind. To this day Oriental travellers express their wonder at the accuracy with which the minutest details of a lesson can be reproduced long afterwards in the exact words of the teacher.

But the great safeguard lay in the constitution of the language itself. In Hebrew, as in all Semitic dialects, *the main root idea of a word was quite intelligible from the consonants alone.* For example,

D B R represented the idea of speaking, and according to the different vowels supplied D_aB_aR, D_iB_eR, $D_oB_{ee}R$, &c., would mean to speak, to say, to address, to converse with, to woo, to promise, to be promised; also, as a noun, a speaker, a word, a commandment, a proposal, a chronicle, and so on.

But it may be objected, even with this root-idea expressed, how was the reader without vowel points to know the exact meaning intended, when each word might be read in so many different ways?

I answer, that even apart from the wonderful memory of the scholars, *the context would, in almost every case, be a sufficient guide to any intelligent reader.* No doubt it is possible to read a vowelless Hebrew word in different ways *if it stand alone;* but in its proper context it is quite a different matter. Even in English, with the great disadvantage of having no fixed root meaning expressed by the consonants, vowelless words are often quite intelligible when read in their proper context. A rapid shorthand writer seldom puts in a vowel, and he can read his notes with ease long after they have been made. Or, to give an easier instance, suppose you have before you the Twenty-third Psalm without vowels—

TH LRD S M SHPHRD I SHLL NT WNT

H MKTH M T L DN N GRN PSTRS

H LDTH M BSD TH STLL WTRS.

When you have once been taught the true reading,

if you be ordinarily familiar with the passage, you will have little or no difficulty in reading it again. Nay more, though each single word in it is capable of being differently read, yet let the experiment be tried, and you will find it almost impossible to make sense of these three lines if you put the wrong vowels to even a single word in them. In Hebrew, owing to its fixed root meanings, this is much more the case.

Of course this is not always so. Very often different readings of a word will make equally good sense, and this is where the reader is entirely dependent on the Jewish tradition as handed down to us in the present vowel points. There is a good illustration in Gen. xlvii. 31, where "Israel bowed himself on the *bed's head*," though the Epistle to the Hebrews (chap. xi. 21), quoting this verse from the Septuagint (Greek) translation, makes him bow "upon the top of his *staff.*" The original word is ΠΜΤΤΗ. By the Hebrews it was read H_aM_iTT_aH, the bed; by the Greek translators, H_aM_aTT_eH, the staff; and it is very hard to say which is the correct reading. Both make equally good sense. Thus it will be seen how mistakes might occur through this method of consonant-writing, and the danger would, of course, be much increased if the old Hebrew manuscripts were written, as they probably were, like the old Greek ones,[1] without any division

[1] The mistakes of the Septuagint translation in dividing what ought to be a single word, or connecting into one words that ought to be separate, give several indications that this was so; yet, on the other

between the words. For example, as if we should write in English Gen. i. 1 :—

NTHBGNNNGGDCRTDTHHVNSNDTHRTH.

The difficulty, however, is not of much practical importance. Indeed, so little is it felt, that to this day not only the Synagogue-rolls, but most modern Jewish writings, books, and newspapers are without the vowel points, and a Hebrew scholar can read them with perfect ease.

If, in addition to what has been now said, the reader will keep in mind (1.) the scrupulous care of the Jews about the accurate reading of their Scriptures; (2.) the fact that, being "people of one book," they were many of them as familiar with the words of their Bible as we are with those of the Lord's Prayer and the Creed; (3.) and that, besides this, there was, as we shall see, a special guild of scribes, at least from the time of Ezra, to preserve and hand down the correct reading, it will be easily seen that the danger from Hebrew consonant-writing is by no means as great as it appears at first sight.

IV.

Grammar and Theology.

It is worth a short digression to tell of the sharp theological contests in Reformation days on this

hand, the Moabite Stone and the Siloam inscriptions, which are very ancient, have the words separated by little round dots cut in the stone, as may be seen by examining frontispiece, and the same division exists in the Pentateuch of the Samaritans.

subject of the Hebrew vowels. Nothing less would suffice the Jewish commentators and grammarians of the time than that these vowel marks had been given, if not to Adam in Paradise, certainly to Moses on Mount Sinai, or, at the very utmost stretch of liberality, that they had been fixed by Ezra and "the men of the Great Synagogue." "They were a revelation from God;" "the consonant letters were the body, and the vowel points the soul, and they move together as an army moves with its leader." Christian scholars knew little about the matter, and quite believed that the vowels were as ancient as the consonants. We can imagine then what a sensation was produced when Elias Levita, a very famous Hebrew scholar, about the year 1540, proved to the world that these vowel marks were not in existence for hundreds of years after the time of our Lord ![1]

Here was a new apple of discord in the already sufficiently discordant field of controversy, whose noise was filling the world in those Reformation days. It is hard to seek the truth dispassionately at such times. Though Luther and Calvin held to the old opinion, the Protestants in general thought they saw a weapon for themselves in Levita's discovery, and, carried away by their theological bias, they sided largely with the new doctrine, and disclaimed the antiquity of the vowel points. Thus they considered they were leaving themselves freer in the interpretation of the Old Testament, throwing off the tradition of the Rabbis, as they

[1] See footnote, chap. viii. p. 102.

had already thrown off the tradition of the Fathers of the Church.

All very satisfactory no doubt to the Reformers. It was rather suspicious, though, in the midst of their satisfaction, to find that the astute controversialists of Rome were quite as much delighted with the new theory as they were, though for a very different reason. "Why," said they, "it is a conclusive proof of our position against you Protestants as to the use of private judgment in interpreting the Bible. God gave His inspired Word in that form without vowel points, so that none but His appointed Church and its accredited teachers could rightly read or understand it; thus were the vulgar people kept from reading it by the special providence of God, lest it should be trodden under foot of swine." "It proves," said the Jesuit Morinus, "that without the infallible interpretation of the Church, the Bible is but a nose of wax, that may be turned any way by ignorant men."

This was indeed turning the tables with a vengeance. Henceforth, as may be supposed, the Reformers were not quite so eager in arguing against the antiquity and value of the vowel points. The reader will better understand the merits of the controversy after he has read the chapters on the story of the Hebrew text, but it may be well to state here that the question is quite a settled one. Nobody now dreams of doubting the comparatively recent origin of the Hebrew vowel points.

V.

Similar Letters.

There is another peculiarity also to be noticed as a common cause of errors in the Old Testament. I mean the similarity of certain pairs of Hebrew letters. Here are two ׳ ׀ which differ only in the length of the tail. The first is the letter Yod, referred to in Matt. v. 18, and corresponds to our Y. The other is the Hebrew w. Clearly, in copying a long difficult manuscript one of these letters might easily be written for the other. A good instance occurs in Ps. xxii. 16, "They pierced my hands and my feet," where this mistake has been the subject of many a controversy (see specimen, p. 204).

Another pair of these similar letters is ר and ד, differing only in the rounding of the angle. They correspond to our R and D. They are responsible for a curious little slip, which the Revisers seem not to have noticed, in Gen. x. 3, 4, and 1 Chron. i. 6, 7. In the first we read Riphat and Dodanim, in the other Diphat and Rodanim. But, indeed, they are responsible for a great many slips. I doubt if there is a more mischievous pair of letters in any alphabet in the world than this same pair. They are continually being mistaken one for the other. There is a disputed reading in 2 Sam. viii. 13, which interestingly exhibits this confusion. It tells of David "smiting of Syria in the Valley of Salt eighteen thousand men. And he put garrisons in Edom." Now this is almost certainly a mistake, even though the Revisers have not corrected it. For the word "Syria" we should read "Edom." The Valley of Salt was in the neighbourhood of *Edom*, not Syria; and if we turn to the parallel passage in 1 Chron. xviii. 12, we read that "Abishai the son of Zeruiah smote of *Edom* in the Valley of Salt eighteen thousand men. And he put garrisons in Edom." The title also of Ps. lx. tells that it was sung when Joab returned, and smote *Edom* in the Valley of Salt.

Now how did this error arise? The words Syria and Edom do not seem very likely to be mistaken one for the other.

But here are the Hebrew forms—

$$\text{אֲרָם} = \text{A R}_a\text{M} = \text{Syria.}$$
$$\text{אֱדֹם} = \text{A}_e\text{D}_o\text{M} = \text{Edom.}$$

It will be seen how easily "Edom" might have become "Syria" by the scribe slightly rounding the angle of the ד.

The Septuagint version has a very curious instance of this error. In 1 Sam. xix. 13, where Michal, to facilitate her husband's escape, put an image in the bed and at its head "a pillow of goats" (hair), the Septuagint translators have "Michal put at his head a *liver* of goats." This shows that they read *Kabhed*, a liver, instead of *Kebhir*, a pillow, confusing the final *d* and *r*. Curiously enough, Josephus [1] follows them in this, "Michal," he says, "having let David down

---

[1] Ant. vi. 11, 4.

B

by a cord out of a window, fitted up a sick bed for him, and *put under the bed-clothes a goat's liver*, and made them believe, by the leaping of the liver, which caused the bed-clothes to move also, that David breathed like an asthmatic man!"

There are also other similar pairs כ ב K B, נ ג G N, ה ח II CH, any of which might by a little carelessness in writing lead to a good deal of confusion;[1] but there is no need of illustrating further.

I have dealt here only with the more modern writing, but when it is added that in the ancient writing also this similarity existed between certain pairs of letters, the reader will understand how, in the long course of ages, errors might easily occur, even with the most anxious care about the accuracy of the text.

VI.

The "Guardians of the Lines."

The ancient scribes, too, had a peculiar trick in writing their manuscripts. In our writing, if a word near the end of the line is too long, we carry part on to the next line, with a hyphen connecting. They never did that. If they were near the end of the line, and the next word was a little too long, they

---

[1] A friend has just pointed out to me an unintentional illustration of this danger in the specimen of Hebrew facing p. 1, where the printer has put in the bottom line קרא in mistake for קרא and two lines higher up אתד instead of אחד being misled by the similarity of the middle letters. I leave the error uncorrected.

took it down unbroken to the line below. But it would not do to leave the blank thus caused at the end of the line. So they filled it up with some other letters, usually those at the beginning of the long word that had been moved down. These letters are called the "Guardians of the Lines." There was just a chance, of course, that a stupid copyist might sometimes blunder over these, especially if the letters could by any possibility be mistaken for any part of the previous word, and so errors might arise in the manuscripts.

Sometimes also a word of frequent occurrence was abbreviated by writing only the first letters, with a few small dashes after it to mark the abbreviation. As, for example, the word YEHOVAH appeared sometimes as Y''. The Septuagint version was thus led into a mistake in translating Jer. vi. 11, where it found CHAMATH YEHOVAH, "the wrath of Jehovah," contracted into CHAMATH Y''. This is very like the form CHAMATHY, which means "my wrath," and they accordingly so translate it.

CHAPTER III.

WHAT IS BIBLICAL CRITICISM?

I.

Mistakes in the Manuscripts.

The sources of error mentioned in the previous chapter are peculiar to the Old Testament manuscripts. But besides those, they were exposed to other sources of error, in common with all manuscripts that have been extensively copied. However careful the scribe may be, it is almost impossible in copying any long difficult manuscript to escape errors of various kinds. Sometimes he will mistake one word for another that looks very like it; sometimes, if having the manuscript read to him, he will confound two words of similar sound; sometimes, after writing in the last word of a line or period, on looking up again, his eye will catch the same word at the end of the next line or period, and he will go on from that, omitting the whole passage between. This last is a very frequent fault. Remarks and explanations, too, written in the margin, will sometimes in transcribing get inserted in the text.

Again, in ancient manuscripts, where there is often no division between the words, each line presenting a continuous row of letters, it might easily happen that one word would be wrongly divided into two, or two combined into one, as in the old story of the infidel who wrote over his bed "God is nowhere," which was read by his little boy as "God is now here." For example, in the end of Ps. xlviii. 14, "This God is our God for ever and ever: He will be our guide unto death," some Hebrew manuscripts have HL-MTH = *unto death*, others HLMTH = *for ever*.

There is no need of further pursuing this subject. The reader who remembers his own frequent slips and erasures, even in writing an ordinary short letter, will easily think of many ways besides in which errors may arise, and will see at once the improbability of the Old Testament manuscripts having escaped absolutely flawless through a transmission of thousands of years. If, even with all the advantages of the printing-press and its multitudes of trained proof-readers, many discrepancies exist between the different editions of our Authorised Version, how can we wonder that it should be so when every copy had to be made by the slow laborious process of writing it out letter by letter?

True, God might have quite obviated this danger. He might have miraculously preserved the original autographs of the inspired writers as a standard by which copies could be corrected for ever, or He might have directed the minds and fingers of Bible-copyists before printing was invented, and of printers and compositors in after days, so as to secure this perfect transmission. If He had seen fit thus to make fallible

men infallible, of course He could have done so.   But
it does not seem to be God's way anywhere to work
miracles for men where their own careful use of the
abilities He has given would suffice for the purpose.
And the Old Testament text is no exception to this
rule.   We shall find, as we go on, that never was a
book guarded with such scrupulous awe and reverence ;
never did any writing come down through the ages so
pure as we have reason to believe did our Hebrew
Bible ; but that it has come to us word for word as it
left the hands of the inspired writers long ago, the
evidence will by no means allow us to believe.

II.

Biblical Criticism.

Biblical criticism is the science which deals with
the discovering and correcting of these errors in the
text.   To be accurate, it should rather be called *Textual
Criticism*, for of course it deals equally with the *text* of
any manuscript, whether Biblical or not, and I shall
generally use this more accurate term in future.[1]   The
reader must not be frightened at the hard name of
this science, as if it meant something abstruse and
difficult to understand.   It may sometimes mean what
is very simple indeed, and instances of it may occur even
in the reading of the daily newspaper.   For example,
I remember somewhere reading of a naval pensioners'
banquet, at which the toast was proposed, " That the

---

[1] I retain the name Biblical Criticism on the title-pages and some
other places, where the more technical expression would be inadvisable.

man who has lost one eye in the service of his country may never see with the other." Well, it did not require much cleverness to suspect a mistake here, and to think of examining another account, and find that the word "distress" or some such word had been omitted from the text. Yet this was an operation in textual criticism, though certainly an operation of the most simple kind.[1] One rather like it in the Bible, but very much more difficult, occurred in the revision of the well-known First Lesson for Christmas Day (Isa. ix.). The old reading is (verse 3), "Thou hast multiplied the nation and *not* increased the joy ; they joy before Thee according to the joy in harvest," &c. Now, in a jubilant passage of this kind, the "not increased their joy" rather jars on one, and this fact led to the examining of a great many old manuscripts and versions of Isaiah, when it was found by the Revisers that the word "not" was most probably a copyist's mistake (see specimen, Book iii. p. 206).

But the operations of textual criticism are not

---

[1] To give a more commonplace example still. The writer had a rather amusing experience in textual criticism a few days since, while travelling in a railway-carriage from Dublin to Kingstown. Right over the carriage-window was the printed direction, " AIT UNTIL THE PAIN STOPS !" It looked Irish to be sure, but somehow did not seem a very probable direction to have been issued by a solemn board of railway directors. A very slight examination showed that a letter, w, had been lost before the first word, and a T before the fourth ; and furthermore, it soon became evident that the P of this word PAIN was originally an R, whose tail had been erased by some mischievous school-boy for a tempting emendation of the reading. And so the extra-ordinary legend resolved itself into the very prosaic advice " WAIT UNTIL THE TRAIN STOPS ; " but the process of thus recovering the correct reading was a true process of textual criticism.

always by any means so simple as this. Sometimes the highest skill of the most experienced critics is utterly at fault. And even in cases like those given above, simple as they seem, the making of such corrections is often a very dangerous experiment. For an expression may seem to the critic incongruous or improbable through his misapprehending the thought that was in the writer's mind. If, then, he should find a number of ancient manuscripts which, owing to the same misapprehension, have ventured to so alter the passage that it agrees with his view, he is clearly in danger of being confirmed in his mistake.

Thus it will be seen textual criticism needs to be wisely and cautiously used. It is an " edge tool," which, the proverb says, children and fools must not play with—many such have played with it to the sore disfiguring of their work—but which in the hands of the skilful workman may do much, and has done much, especially during the past century, in removing blemishes from the Bible text. In applying to the Bible, it requires a calm judicial mind, reverent towards God's Word, skilled in the accurate weighing of evidence, and through long study of manuscripts well acquainted with the many ways in which copyists' errors are likely to arise.

III.
Its Axioms and Rules.

Its rules, even when they seem to the uninitiated difficult and unreasonable, are simply the conclusions

of common sense founded on a special knowledge of
the subject. For example, that in certain cases where
we have to decide between two different readings of
a passage, " *the more difficult reading is to be preferred
to the easier,* " merely means that experience of manuscripts has taught the critic that copyists are more
likely to try to simplify a difficult passage than to
complicate one that already runs freely and easily, and
therefore the more difficult reading is likely to be
the correct one.[1] So also the rule that " *the shorter
of two readings is to be preferred to the more wordy,*"
means only that experience has likewise taught that
copyists are more inclined to expand a short terse
reading than to condense a more wordy one.

For our present inquiry it is only necessary to
trouble the reader with three very simple and self-
evident propositions of textual criticism :—

(1.) *If manuscripts were all of equal value, the truth
might be expected, of course, to be with the majority*—
e.g., if out of seventy manuscripts, sixty contained a
certain reading and ten omitted it, that reading would
probably be correct.

(2.) *But manuscripts are not all of the same value.*
For illustration, let o represent the original document,

---

[1] For example, I am informed that in the hymn "Rock of Ages,"
the line "when mine eyelids close in death" reads in some copies
"when mine eyestrings burst in death." This is clearly the more
"difficult" reading, but for that reason it is the most likely to be the
original one, since nobody would be likely to alter the other for such
an unpleasant reading, but any one might be tempted to change it for
the other.

and A and B copies of equal value made from it. Now suppose three copies further to be made from B, and from these again any numbers of others. It is clear that the evidence of the one copy, A, would be worth that of the whole set, c, d, e, 1, 2, 3, 4, 5, 6, 7, copies descended from B.

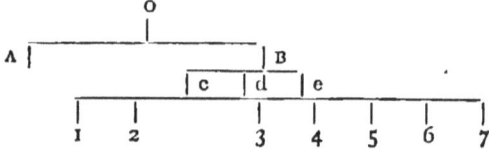

(3.) *The earlier any manuscript, the more likely it is to be correct.* For in the many ways we have referred to it is possible for errors to creep into the first copy of a manuscript. Any such errors would, of course, be repeated by the man that afterwards copied from this, who would also sometimes add other errors of his own. This would be equally true of the man who copied from him, and so on all the way down. So that clearly as copies increased errors would be likely to increase with them, and therefore, as a general rule, the earlier manuscripts would be the more correct ones.[1]

IV.

Its Working Material.

The evidence on which the textual criticism of the Old Testament chiefly bases its judgments I have roughly divided into two parts :—

[1] Of course this is only a general rule. It is quite possible that a manuscript of the present year should be copied *direct* from one 1500 years old, and therefore be more correct than many which have existed for centuries.

I. THE OLD HEBREW MANUSCRIPTS, *i.e.*, copies of the Sacred Books made in the original language. These are the foundation on which everything rests.

II. THE OTHER OLD DOCUMENTS to aid in the testing and correcting of these manuscripts. Under this head come—(1.) The Ancient Versions, *i.e.*, the translations of the Hebrew books into other languages long ago. (2.) The quotations from the Bible in ancient Jewish commentaries, to which we may add the earlier printed editions of the Hebrew Bible, made perhaps from older manuscripts than any that have survived.

Accordingly this volume is divided into three parts—

Book I. The "Old Hebrew Documents," and the question of Biblical Criticism.

Book II. The "Other Old Documents," and their aid in Biblical Criticism.

Book III. The New Bible a specimen of Biblical Criticism, to illustrate how the above materials are used in removing blemishes from the Bible text.

CHAPTER IV.

I.

Some Curious Old Manuscripts.

We are now in a position to glance at the old Hebrew manuscripts of the Bible at present available to scholars. There are very many of them—nearly two thousand have already been examined—strange and curious old documents, on rough cumbrous hides, on brown African skins, on rolls of the most delicate parchment, some of them mildewed and faded and torn, some almost as fresh as on the day when they were made. From all quarters of the earth they come, from Palestine and Babylon and the distant East, from Africa and the islands of the Indian Sea, from the great universities and libraries of the Gentiles, from the filthy Jewish Ghettos in Italy and Spain. There are the fine synagogue parchments, with their exquisite writing wrought out with continual fasting and prayer; here the curious manuscripts of the Rabbis of China, and the rough red goatskin rolls from the black Jews of Malabar;[1] piles of shrivelled fragments of only a

[1] In the early times there were Jewish settlements in India and China, and Hebrew scholars often turned their attention in that direc-

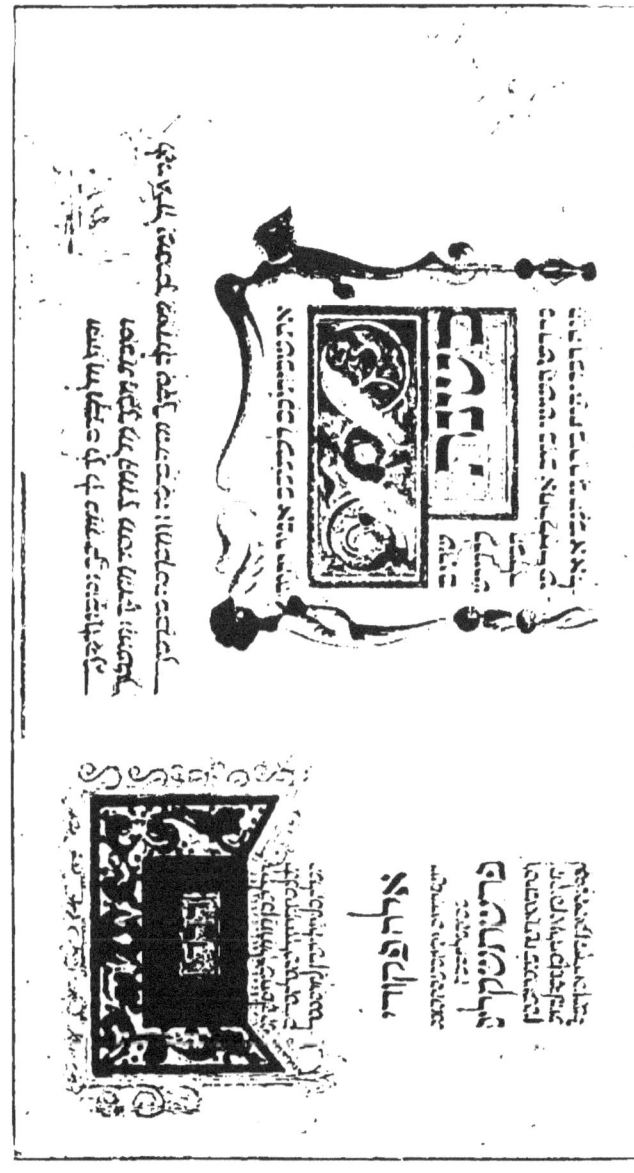

SPECIMENS OF MEDIEVAL HEBREW MANUSCRIPTS.

(Photographed by kind permission of Professor Westwood of Oxford, from the Paleographia Sacra Pictoria.)

To face page 28.

few pages, and rough leathern rolls 150 feet long; beautiful book-shaped copies of the Law, and soiled and faded sheets of the Prophets and the Psalms, disinterred from the " Ghenizas," where the Jews had buried them. Many a romantic story doubtless belongs to the history of these silent sheets and the names of the forgotten writers, which some of them bear.   Stories of battle and siege, as of the capture of Toledo by Edward the Black Prince, where the famous " Codex Ezræ " [1] was found amongst the spoils ; stories of life in the old Jewish academies long ago ; stories of fierce persecution, of brave endurance ; of men fleeing with their scriptures from the " followers of Christ ; " of holocausts of ancient Jewish manuscripts of the Bible ; of blazing synagogues and ruined homes,

> " And dead white faces upturned to the sky,
>   Calling for vengeance to their fathers' God."

---

tion.   In 1806 Dr. Buchanan obtained, among other manuscripts, a roll of the Pentateuch from the black Jews of Malabar.   It is now in the University Library at Cambridge.   It consists of about thirty-five goatskins dyed red.   It is the breadth of the Jewish sacred cubit, and when complete must have been nearly ninety feet long.

[1] The Jews of Toledo, in the Middle Ages, had in their synagogues a roll called the Codex Ezræ, or the Codex Azaræ.   Some believed it to have belonged to Ezra ; others thought it was the copy deposited in the'Azara or Hall of the Temple (see p. 81), and preserved in the siege and capture of Jerusalem.   At the capture of Toledo by Edward the Black Prince in 1367, it came into his possession as part of the spoils. The Jews redeemed it for a large sum, but it was afterwards destroyed by fire with the synagogue.   So highly was it valued, that manuscripts were sent from all places to be compared with it, and some of our existing manuscripts have appended to them a certificate that they have been compared, not directly with the Codex Ezræ itself, but with manuscripts that had been verified by comparison with it.

But the very existence itself of these manuscripts has sufficient in it of wonder and romance. They are the holy oracles of God written in the " holy tongue " of His people, faithfully handed down from generation to generation since the days of the thunderings and lightnings of Sinai. Who can look on them without reverence and awe and deep conviction of the truth of revelation ? Who can think without emotion of that poor, despised, hunted race, through all the ages preserving for their persecutors the message of Jehovah ? Surely enough of wonder and romance that those records should have come down to us from the days of Moses ; that in this world of shortlived races, rapidly succeeding each other and passing away, there should remain one mysterious people existing to this day from the dawn of history, the guardians through thirty centuries of the words in those old Hebrew scrolls !

II.

A Perplexing Discovery.

But what is the value to the textual critic of these venerable documents ? How many thousand years do they go back ? Have we amongst them the autograph of any inspired writer ? Have we manuscripts at least of the time of our Lord ? How far do they enable us to fix with certainty the exact original of the Hebrew Old Testament ?

To the reader who knows something of the New Testament writings, with their documents reaching up near the days of the Apostles, and the many variations nevertheless existing in the text, an acquaintance with these strange old manuscripts can scarcely fail to cause surprise. Not one of them, we shall see immediately, is written in the ancient writing. This, perhaps, he might have expected from what has been already said. But, as he inquires further, a very perplexing fact indeed reveals itself. He finds—

I. THAT THE OLDEST HEBREW MANUSCRIPT IN EXISTENCE IS OF DATE LITTLE EARLIER THAN WILLIAM THE CONQUEROR!

II. AND THAT IN ALL THE HEBREW MANUSCRIPTS THAT HAVE EVER BEEN EXAMINED, THE TEXT IS ALMOST WORD FOR WORD THE SAME!

Let us realise what this means. (1.) That of the early Old Testament books, written more than 3000 years ago, we have not a single copy 1000 years old ; or, in other words, that the earliest Old Testament manuscript in existence is as far from the time of the original writers as would be a New Testament manuscript written to-day. (2.) That amid all the copyists' errors and variations, which are the common fate of every ancient book—the New Testament included— this most ancient of all the books of the world has virtually no variations at all !

III.

The Guardianship of the Bible.

Now, how are these strange phenomena to be explained ? This question will be fully treated in the following story of the manuscripts, but a brief summary of the answer here will perhaps enable the reader to follow it more intelligently. The popular notion is that of an absolutely perfect guardianship of the Hebrew text by the Jews. Their deep reverence for their Scriptures and the scrupulous care with which these Scriptures were handed down is considered quite sufficient explanation for this marvellous agreement of manuscripts. Well, there is much truth in this, a good deal more, we venture to say, than is believed by many of those who question the accuracy of the Hebrew Old Testament. We shall see as we go on that for nearly 2000 years past at least this guardianship was almost perfect; scarcely a single important slip of a transcriber could have occurred without detection in all the copying of manuscripts during that time. But we cannot speak thus confidently of the manuscripts of the earlier period. They certainly were not all uniform. The manuscripts used by the Palestine Jews varied, often considerably, from those of the "Jews of the Dispersion" in other lands. The Palestine manuscripts themselves had some variations between them. Therefore some better explanation must be found for the uniformity in the existing Hebrew manuscripts.

IV.

An Ancient Revision.

We must first clearly distinguish between the Palestine manuscripts and all others. The Palestine text is that which has come down to us, and, as will be seen, we have every reason to consider that it has come down to us substantially correct. We do not believe that it is entirely free from copyists' errors, but from what we know of the solemn reverence with which it has been always regarded from the beginning, and the scrupulous, almost superstitious care with which it has been transmitted for the past two thousand years, we have ample reason to believe that this Palestine Old Testament has come down to us very nearly as it left the hands of the original writers.

This, however, does not sufficiently account for the almost word-for-word agreement between our existing manuscripts, since, as we have seen, even the Palestine manuscripts in ancient times were not without some variation. Unless by a continual miracle, no writings could have passed through the process of copying and recopying for thousands of years without many an error and variation arising.

The explanation is by no means easy to find. The following chapters will tell of a long continual revision carried on through many centuries by the ablest Jewish scholars ; of a mysterious standard text set up, to which every manuscript conformed; of the existence of all Hebrew Bibles in the famous " days of the Massoretes " in this uniform state in which they appear to-day. This uniform text was then fixed and stereotyped as the " Textus Receptus " or standard text of the Old Testament. It is known as the " Massoretic " text, and our manuscripts are all " Massoretic " manuscripts.

C

It is well for the reader to remember this name. We have much to say of it afterwards in the " Story of the Manuscripts."

V.

The Vanished Manuscripts.

But what of the disappearance of the very ancient manuscripts? Why have we none even a thousand years old? If divergent copies once existed, why is there not one to be found to-day to break the uniformity of the Massoretic text? It is generally answered that the Jews destroyed all copies that varied from the standard Massoretic Bible. And this may well have been so. We know that in a like case, when the Caliph Othman adopted a standard text of the Koran, he destroyed every copy that differed from it. The text of the Vedas, too, in India, appears to have been revised about five hundred years before Christ, and no divergent copy allowed afterwards to remain. This may have happened in the case of the ancient Jewish manuscripts.

But there is really no need of postulating such a cause. Why should they not have vanished as Jewish manuscripts are continually vanishing now? If the present Jewish customs existed long ago, they must have made the survival of any very ancient manuscript well nigh impossible. Even those which we possess to-day have only escaped through having fallen into Gentile hands. It is a rigid rule to this day among

PART OF THE ILLUMINATED TITLES OF THE BOOKS OF ECCLESIASTES AND NUMBERS.

From a Fifteenth Century Hebrew Manuscript.

On the reverse of the last leaf is written this deed of sale :—"To testify and make it appear to Rabbi Jachiel, the son of Uri, I acknowledge that I have delivered to him this Pentateuch, of which I have received the value in ready money, and the sale thereof is an ever lasting sale. Done this 4th day, the 28th of the month Ejar, A.M. 5229. The words of Jacob the son of Mordecai."

the Jews that manuscripts condemned from any cause
as unfit for use must be forthwith reverently destroyed
lest they should fall into the hands of the profane.
Now, manuscripts were condemned for very slight
defects ; a new sheet if there were found in it three
errors of the scribe, a synagogue roll if injured through
the wear and tear of rolling and unrolling for the
daily lessons, or if letters were blurred or effaced
through the custom of kissing the opening and closing
words of the portion to be read. A "Gheniza" was
usually attached to the synagogue, a place where
these condemned manuscripts were reverently buried ;
though, by the way, this did not always save them
from defilement, for it appears from the Catalogues that
at least two decayed old parchments in the library of
the great Hebrew scholar, De Rossi, were unearthed at
Lucca from one of these Ghenizas.

VI.

Are our Manuscripts Correct?

In any case, however we explain the disappearance
of the ancient copies, one thing is clear, that, as far as
Hebrew manuscripts are concerned, we are shut up to
this Massoretic text. We have no other. The makers
of the Authorised Version simply translate it, with rarely
any question of its absolute correctness. The recent
revisers, while expressing their doubts, think it "most
prudent to adopt the Massoretic text as the basis of
their work, and to depart from it, as the Authorised

translators had done, only in exceptional cases." Therefore it becomes a most important question, How far do
these Massoretic manuscripts correctly reproduce the
very words of the Old Testament writers, and where
they fail in so doing is there any means of discovering
and correcting their errors ?   The answer to this question also, as far as it can be given, must be gathered
from the following " Story of the Manuscripts."

CHAPTER V.

THE EARLY AGES.

I.

What can we Learn of the Vanished Manuscripts?

The first trace of the documents of the Old Testament is found in Exod. xvii. 14, where, after the battle with Amalek, we are told that Moses was commanded to "write it in a book," either the original manuscript of part of the Pentateuch or one of the sources from which the Pentateuch was afterwards compiled.[1] It is a "far cry" from that manuscript of Rephidim, three thousand years ago, to the Hebrew documents in our hands to-day. We have to learn now what is known

---

[1] There is no doubt that many previously existing documents were used in the composition of the Old Testament books, the Genealogies, the "Book of the Wars of Jehovah," the "Book of Iddo," the "Book of Jasher," the "Chronicles of the Kings of Judah and Israel," &c. But the discussion of this question, deeply interesting as it is, lies quite outside our present plan. The reader will clearly understand that this little book deals only with the *external* history of the Jewish Bible, *i.e.*, the preservation and transmission of the books as they have come down to us. With their composition and internal history, and the whole fascinating but difficult question of what is called the "higher criticism," we have nothing to do here.

of the history of the text during all the centuries between.

It is but very little, reader, that there is to learn, especially of the earlier ages, and even that little can be but lightly touched on in a simple popular treatise such as the present. We may roughly divide the history into four periods :—

I. THE EARLY AGES, from Moses to Ezra, *i.e.*, to about B.C. 500.

II. EZRA AND THE SCRIBES, to the destruction of Jerusalem, A.D. 70.

III. THE TALMUD PERIOD, to about A.D. 500.

IV. THE DAYS OF THE MASSORETS, to A.D. 1000.

Let us try to investigate the subject by examining the text as far as we can at each period of its history. First, then, we inquire, At the close of the " Early Ages " did all the copies agree in every letter, and was the text absolutely correct as it left the hands of the inspired writers ?

II.

Call our First Witness—The Sacred Books.

Of this first period little is known except what we can learn from the books themselves. There are no manuscripts of that period remaining, no history, no collateral sources of information, except perhaps the Samaritan Pentateuch, to be afterwards examined.

What, then, we inquire, can be learned from the books themselves ?   What of the text of these vanished manuscripts? Did it agree exactly with that which has come down to us? Was it carefully guarded from corruption of copyists? And the little that we can gather of an answer to our question is something to this effect:—

The manuscripts were written in the ancient Hebrew writing on rolls of linen or papyrus, or skins fastened together, much like the present parchment rolls of the synagogue. [We read, for example, of the Roll of the Book (Ps. xl. 7), Jeremiah's Roll (Jer. xxxvi. 14), and the Flying Roll of Zechariah's vision (Zech. v. 1).] They were guarded with the most reverent care, especially the Mosaic writings, the only Bible which the Jews possessed for centuries. Moses, we are told, committed his original manuscript "unto the priests, the sons of Levi, which bare the Ark of the Covenant, and unto all the elders of Israel; and he commanded the Levites to take the book, and to put it by (not *in*) the side of the Ark of the Covenant, to be there for a witness against the people of Israel" (Deut. xxxi. 9, 24, 26). It was preserved, therefore, in the Holy of Holies, guarded by the awful majesty of God's visible presence. Every seven years this "Book of the Law" was to be read before the people; and in Joshua's days we learn (Joshua viii. 35) that "there was not a word of all that Moses commanded which Joshua read not before all the congregation." Further, it was enjoined that every king of Israel, soon after his accession, should write out with his own hands a copy from this manuscript, which was kept by the priests and

Levites (Deut. xvii. 18); and it seems to have become part of the coronation ceremonies that this original document, or at least a copy of it, should be placed in the hands of the king when he was crowned (2 Kings xi. 12, and 2 Chron. xxiii. 11). The frequent mention of this "Book of the Law" as that which must be taught to men as God's guide for their life will occur to every reader.

We find the statement in the early Christian fathers, Tertullian, Epiphanius, St. Augustine, and others, that the other inspired books also were placed in the sanctuary, and what is of more consequence, Josephus, the Jewish historian, seems to confirm this assertion.[1] The Bible also lends it some support. We read in Joshua xxiv. 26, that Joshua added on his own writing to the " Book of the Law ; " and in 1 Sam. x. 25, that Samuel " told the people the manner of the kingdom, and wrote it in the book, and *laid it up before the Lord.*" So that, altogether, there seems reason to believe that the Tabernacle, and afterwards the Temple, was the regular depository of the sacred manuscripts.

In Samuel's days the original documents (*i.c.*, the Law at least, and perhaps some of the other books) would naturally be kept with the Ark in Shiloh, the home of the priests and of sacred learning.

[1] See "Antiquities," Book iii. 1. 7, and Book v. 1. 17. He speaks also ("Life of Josephus," § 75) of having, by the favour of Titus, saved the "Holy Writings" at the destruction of Jerusalem (probably the Temple manuscripts of the other books) ; and in the " Jewish Wars " (vii. v. 5) he tells that the Law, taken from the Temple, was borne aloft in the triumph of Titus and placed in the Palace.

But it would seem as if the growing degeneracy of the priesthood and their loss of influence in the nation necessitated now the calling forth of a new order to guard the Divine deposit and communicate its contents to the people. We find all Samuel's teaching based upon these Scripture records, and probably, that the knowledge of them might be preserved and disseminated, he founded his theological colleges or " Schools of the Prophets," where picked young scholars were trained in the sacred learning at Naioth and Gilgal and Bethel.

We find Elijah visiting these schools in later days as he passed to his miraculous assumption, and afterwards his successor, Elisha, moving amongst them preparing and exhorting these young teachers of the future.[1]

The chief work of the students no doubt would be the study and expounding and copying of the Law, though sacred poetry and music were also an important part of their course.

And not only were they the expounders and guardians of the older Scripture, but also as God inspired them, the authors of the new. They were the national poets and annalists, the composers of psalms, the compilers of records such as the Books of Nathan and Gad and Iddo the seer, so valuable afterwards as materials for the Old Testament history. Two of the oldest of the prophetical books, Hosea and Jonah, were the work of men trained in the schools of Elijah, and

[1] See 1 Sam. xix. 19, 20 ; 2 Kings ii. 3-5, iv. 38, vi. 1, &c.

afterwards no writing was received as inspired unless it could claim a prophet for its author, though not necessarily one trained in prophetical schools.

It is easy to see how this new order of trained students would be a further safeguard to the purity of the text originally committed to the priestly line, and after them, in the days of the Captivity, we find the regularly appointed Guild of the Scribes and the critical study of the manuscripts at least in its beginning.

Before the Captivity, however, we have another glimpse of the guardianship of the " Books "—a revelation of gross neglect and of holy zeal. When Hezekiah began his reign he found the Temple shut up, and its worship and its sacred manuscripts quite disregarded ; and so we are told he gathered together in the East Street the priests and the Levites, and by his burning words he aroused their enthusiasm for restoring the "service of God and the Law and the commandments."

How far those men of Hezekiah went in examining and restoring the Hebrew manuscripts it is impossible to say. In the passing mentions of them, we gather that they devoted themselves in Jerusalem to the study of the Law ;[1] that they found and copied out a considerable part of the Proverbs of Solomon ;[2] that they examined the pile of copies of the Temple Psalms (how vast it must have been when the chief singers

[1] 2 Chron. xxx. 22, xxxi. 4.   [2] Prov. xxv. 1.

numbered two hundred and eighty-eight !),[1] and from
them selected the genuine Psalms of David and Asaph
the seer.[2] Jewish tradition assigns to them also the
copying out of the Books of Isaiah, Ecclesiastes, and
Solomon's Song. However this may be, clearly the
work of the royal reformer and his "men" must
have had an important bearing on the fortunes of the
Jewish Bible.

And then comes a relapse almost to utter Paganism.
The following reigns, with their idolatrous desecration,
brought things to such a pass that a great sensation was caused in the days of Josiah, when Hilkiah
the priest[3] discovered, in some hiding-place, the lost
and almost forgotten "Temple manuscript" of the
Law, concealed probably to escape the rage of the
idolatrous Manasseh.

This certainly looks rather badly for the guardianship of the old manuscripts. And yet I doubt if even
from this one should argue to the probability of their
having become corrupted either by carelessness or
design. The danger here would be rather their being
totally lost. Indeed, at such times, the risk of corruption through copyists' errors would probably be
smaller than ever, since there would be very little
likelihood of any copying at all.

---

[1] 1 Chron. xxv. 7. [2] 2 Chron. xxix. 30.
[3] 2 Chron. xxxiv. 14, &c.

Summary of this Evidence.

It may be well to present this evidence in a more condensed and systematic form, so as to show at a glance what reason we have for believing in the substantial accuracy of the Hebrew manuscripts during this early period.

1. The deep reverence of the Jews for their sacred writings and the care with which they were copied in all the known period of the history of the text may surely be assumed in this its comparatively unknown period as well.

2. With regard to the Mosaic writings at least, the Bible itself abundantly confirms this assumption.

3. The less any manuscript is copied, the less danger, of course, there is of errors in copying. The numerous variations of the New Testament documents are a result of the very extensive demand for copies. There would be but little of this in the early Old Testament days.

4. The preservation and transmission of the text was not left to chance or to untrained men. The early manuscripts were committed to the priestly order under peculiarly solemn circumstances. The trained teachers from the schools of the prophets must have done much in the guarding and copying as well as teaching of the Scripture, and after them in the next period arose the new Guild of the Scribes and the critical study of the Bible manuscripts.

5. The Temple manuscript of the Law brought to
light by Hilkiah, B.C. 623, after its long concealment,
would probably tend to correct any errors in existing
copies and preserve future transcripts from corruption.

6. Though the other books were not regarded with
as high a veneration as the Pentateuch, and therefore
were not so safe from copyists' mistakes, yet, on the
other hand, they were less often copied, not being
used in worship or in teaching the people. Besides,
the prophetic and historical books were not very long
in existence before the great collecting and revising
of the Scriptures, of which we shall hear in the
following chapter. Indeed, some were not written
till after the Captivity, when the jealous guardianship
of the text had already begun.[1]

7. It is worth notice that the inspired prophets,
while sternly rebuking the people for their iniquities,
and the priests for their shortcomings and neglect,
never let fall a word charging them with mutilation
or corruption of the Word of God ; though, of course,
this argument only holds good against serious or wilful
corruption.

We may add, too, that the belief held by the Jews
of our Lord's time on the subject should probably count
for something. It is expressed in the Talmud "that
Moses received the Book of the Law from Sinai, and

[1] It is interesting to note that the Revised Version, restoring the
definite article omitted by the Authorised in Dan. ix. 2, shows us that
the prophetic writings were at that day reverently regarded as "the
Books" or "the Scriptures." Daniel read in "the Books" the prophecy of Jeremiah about the Captivity.

delivered it to Joshua ; Joshua delivered it to the
elders, the elders to the prophets, and the prophets to
the men of the great synagogue, from whom it passed
to the heads of the families of the Scribes." And
Josephus, about the same period, insists, " We have
not an innumerable multitude of books, as the Greeks,
but only twenty-two, which contain the record of all
past times, and which are justly believed to be divine.
. . . During so many ages as have already passed, *no
one has been so bold as to add anything to them or to take
anything from them, or to make any change in them ;* but
it becomes natural to all Jews from their birth to esteem
these books to contain divine doctrines, to persist in
them, and, if occasion be, willingly to die for them." [1]

Such facts as these should go far to prove the
reverence with which the manuscripts were regarded
and the care exercised in their transmission. From
them we gather that God's watchful providence, by
the use of ordinary human means, preserved for us at
least the general purity of the Hebrew text, and the
fullest confirmation of this will meet us as we go on.

But in the case of the New Testament, we know
that, with this *general* purity of the text, there existed
some minor slips and inaccuracies of copyists, such as
have been spoken of in a previous chapter as incidental
to all manuscript-copying, and therefore the question
naturally arises, Did such exist also in the case of the
Old Testament of the " Early Ages ? "

[1] Discourse against Apion, § 8.

IV.

A Search for further Evidence.

The reader will naturally ask, How on earth could such a question be answered? How can we ascertain anything further about the condition of the early text if every early manuscript has perished centuries and centuries ago?

Well, reader, it is not a very easy task, but yet it is not quite impossible either. Suppose that at the close of what we have here called the Early Ages one copy of the existing Hebrew Bible should have been entirely separated off from the rest, carried away to a far-distant land *where there was no possibility of contact with the Palestine copies*, and there become the parent of a long line of manuscripts. Suppose some traveller should find for us to-day a number of manuscript descendants of this solitary Bible which had thus branched off 2500 years ago. Would not the comparing of these with our present manuscripts be a valuable study, and help us much in our inquiry about the early text?

If we found them absolutely agreeing with ours, should we not be right in saying that our Bible is word for word the same as that of Palestine in the Early Ages, and that all the manuscripts of these Early Ages most probably agreed in every letter.

If we found them agreeing substantially with ours, but differing a little here and there in words and turns of expression, perhaps sometimes in adding or omitting a few words in a verse, should we not conclude that certainly our Bible is at least substantially the Bible of the Early Ages, even if it does not correspond in every word and letter. For all in which these two sets of manuscripts agree must infallibly have belonged to the ancient text from which they have both sprung. There is no other possible explanation of their agreement, since, according to our supposition, they could have had no contact with each other. So that the reader will see we might be quite able thus to reproduce with certainty a large part of the ancient text.

But what of the discrepancies between the two? What should we say of them ? Surely this, that one or both of the sets of manuscripts had got some copyists' errors, but at first we could not tell which.

Suppose then, lastly, that, while knowing of the jealous care with which our Scriptures had been guarded, we found from the history of this foreign country that its manuscripts had been very carelessly kept, that at one period at least there had been designedly introduced for political purposes certain of these differences which we had noticed. Should we not be inclined to say that where their readings differed from ours the strange manuscripts were probably corrupt all the way through ; though, of course, we could not say that in all these differences our own copies were certainly right ?

Thus it will be evident—and this is very important

A PAGE FROM ONE OF ARCHBISHOP USSHER'S MANUSCRIPTS OF THE SAMARITAN PENTATEUCH.

to remember—that the bad character of tho strange manuscripts would not weaken their evidence as to the *correctness* of ours in places where both agree, though it would very decidedly weaken their evidence as to the *incorrectness* of ours in places where they differ.

v.

Call our Next Witness, the Samaritan Bible.

Now, in our search for evidence about the ancient text, we come upon one document which satisfies all the above conditions. We discover that there exists a Pentateuch among the Samaritans, a book which was separated from the Jewish Pentateuch manuscripts at the close of the " Early Ages," though only discovered by European scholars in comparatively recent times.

This document is fully dealt with later on (Book ii. p. 118), but it is necessary to refer to it slightly here. Its importance, of course, consists in the fact that it is Samaritan ; that its text has existed separate from that of the Jews since about five hundred years before Christ —at latest, since the time when the renegade, Manasseh, in his passion for his young Samaritan wife, fled from the anger of Nehemiah to be priest in the schismatic temple of the Samaritans at Gerizim,[1] probably carrying with him a copy of the Law. The bitter enmity existing between the two races is ample security that

[1] Neh. xiii. 28. Josephus, Antiquities, Book xi. chaps. vii. and viii., where, however, the story is transferred to a later period.

D

its text has never since been influenced by that of the Jewish Pentateuch; there-fore the whole portion in which it and our Jewish manuscripts of the Pen-tateuch agree, and that means substantially al-most the entire contents, must certainly belong to the " Early Ages " Bible. There is no other way pos-sible of explaining their agreement. So that, it will be seen, *this Samari-tan Pentateuch is a most important witness to the substantial purity of our present text.*

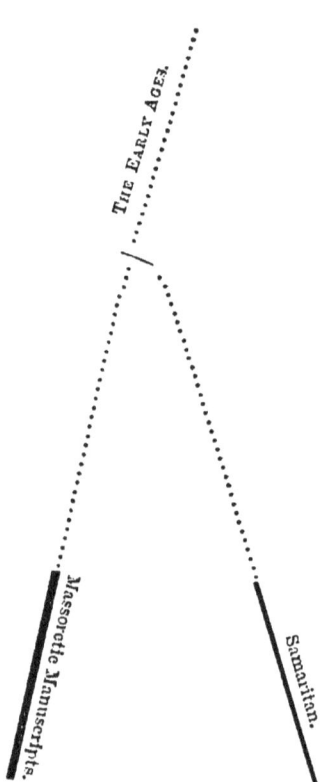

But then the Samari-tan, in certain particulars, is found to differ from our text. The ages of the patriarchs do not agree; the name Ebal, in Deut. xxvii. 4, appears as Gerizim —though this is of little moment, it is so evidently a corruption in favour of the Samaritan temple there ; the narrative is fuller in many particulars, and there are expansions and explanations of passages which seem condensed and difficult in the Jewish Bible.

Now, it has been argued by some that these dis-

crepancies go far to show that at the close of the
Early Ages, when the Samaritan branched off, similar
discrepancies must have existed between the early
manuscripts; that the Samaritan was copied from one
set of manuscripts, the Jewish from another and different set.

If we were as sure of accurate transmission in the
case of the Samaritan as we are in that of the Jewish
Scriptures, this would be a good argument. When
the manuscripts of this Samaritan Pentateuch were
first imported into Europe in the seventeenth century, much surprise was felt at its variations from the
Hebrew, and scholars were at first inclined to give it
a high position. But, on fuller acquaintance, it quite
lost its character, as the reader will see for himself later
on. Suffice it to say here, that it now stands convicted
of having been freely tampered with, not only for controversial purposes, as in the case of Ebal and Gerizim, but
also in many places to remove what seemed difficulties,
and to make the narrative flow more freely and easily.

Therefore we conclude that our Samaritan witness
is not of sufficiently good character; and that, while
its substantial agreement with the Massoretic manuscripts is a strong confirmation of their correctness, its
charge of minor inaccuracies in these Hebrew manuscripts, or of discrepancies existing in the Early Ages,
is, as the Scotch lawyers would say, " not proven."

At the same time, some of its variations are supported by the authority of the Septuagint and other
versions of the following period, and it would be a

bold thing to say that in every little discrepancy
between them the Jewish Bible is certainly right
and the Samaritan certainly wrong.   There are some
few instances at least where we may well doubt this.
For example, we give amongst the "Specimens" in
Book iii. p. 189 a Samaritan addition to the text
of Gen. iv. 8 which is strongly supported by other
authority, and is admitted by the recent revisers into
their margin : "Cain said to Abel his brother, *Let us
go into the field.*"   We have shown in that place that
the Samaritan is very probably right, and that the
words may have at some time fallen out of the Hebrew
text.   In Gen. xlvii. 21 it is almost certainly right
in telling that Joseph *made bondmen* of the Egyptians
for Pharaoh (see Revised Version, margin), instead of
merely "removing" them, as we have it.

But we only listen to it here because other authorities strongly support it.   We repeat again that its
variations from the Hebrew carry little or no weight
with them.   Like all other such witnesses, it has to
suffer for its general bad character even where it may
be in the right.   No scholar would now think of
using its unsupported testimony to call in question
the accuracy of the Hebrew text.

VI.

Cross-Examine our First Witness.

There seems just one other possible way of learning
anything as to the manuscripts of the Early Ages,

and that is by cross-examining, as it were, our first witness, the existing Old Testament itself. There is a certain class of evidence found within its covers which is sometimes brought forward as a proof that in the Early Ages, before the separate books were collected into one Jewish "Bible," and the Canon of the Old Testament closed, the manuscripts must have suffered from careless transcription.

It is that of "repeated passages." What seem to be copies of the same writings are found in two or more different places, and these passages, when closely compared, are found to exhibit variations of more or less importance.

Compare, for example :—

2 Sam. xxii.	with Ps. xviii.
Ps. xiv.	,, Ps. liii.
1 Chr. xvi. 8–22	,, Ps. cv. 1–15.
1 Chr. xvi. 23–33	,, Ps. xcvi.
2 Kings xix., xx.	,, Isa. xxxvii., xxxviii.
2 Kings xxv.	,, Jer. lii.
Isa. xv., xvi.	,, Jer. xlviii.

There are nearly a hundred such instances of parallelism in the Old Testament, easily discovered by means of a good Reference Bible ; and to understand aright the value of their evidence, the reader should examine a few of them for himself before going on. However, as one cannot trust all readers to take this trouble, perhaps we had better print one or two illus-

trations.   Let us take at random the first two pairs
in the above list:—

2 SAM. XXII.	PSALM XVIII.
	I love Thee, O Lord, my strength.
The Lord is my rock, and my fortress, and deliverer ; The God of my rock ; in Him will I trust : My shield, and the horn of my salvation, my high tower, and my refuge, my Saviour ; Thou savest me from violence.	The Lord is my rock, and my fortress, and deliverer ; My God, my strong rock ; in Him will I trust : My shield, and the horn of my salvation, my high tower.
I will call upon the Lord, who is worthy to be praised : So shall I be saved from mine enemies.	I will call upon the Lord, who is worthy to be praised : So shall I be saved from mine enemies.
When the waves of death compassed me, The floods of ungodliness made me afraid ; The cords of Sheol were round about me ; The snares of death came upon me.	The cords of death compassed me, And the floods of ungodliness made me afraid. The cords of Sheol were round about me ; The pains of death came upon me.
In my distress I called upon the Lord, Yea, I called unto my God.	In my distress I called upon the Lord, And cried unto my God.
And He rode upon a cherub and did fly ; Yea, He was seen upon the wings of the wind. And He made darkness pavilions round about Him.	And He rode upon a cherub and did fly ; Yea, He flew swiftly upon the wings of the wind. He made darkness His hiding-place, His pavilion round about Him.

PSALM XIV.	PSALM LIII.
The fool hath said in his heart, There is no God. They are corrupt ; they have done abominable works ; There is none that doeth good. The LORD looked down from heaven upon the children of men, To see if there were any that did understand, That did seek after God.	The fool hath said in his heart, There is no God. Corrupt are they, and have done abominable iniquity. There is none that doeth good. God looked down from heaven upon the children of men, To see if there were any that did understand, That did seek after God.
Have all the workers of iniquity no knowledge ? Who eat up my people as they eat bread, And call not upon the LORD.	Have the workers of iniquity no knowledge ? Who eat up my people as they eat bread, And call not upon God.

In the first of these cases the existence of two separato editions of the same poem is easily understood. A couple of thousand years ago the compilers of the Book of Psalms, the Jewish Church Hymnal, extracted the poem for their collection out of 2 Samuel, or perhaps the author of 2 Samuel copied it from the hymn-book to insert in his story. In after - days this history and this hymn-book were bound between the same covers, and thus we find two separate copies of the poem, and what concerns us most, we find that these two copies do not exactly correspond.

Now, it has been argued that the differences between them point to a corruption of either or both the copies, and as the Bible copyists of later days had grown so extremely scrupulous about the accuracy of the text, therefore the corruption probably belongs to the Early Ages.

But do the discrepancies point to corruption at all ? Not necessarily, I think. In all our present Church Hymnals there are poems selected out of the works of certain authors, and designedly shortened or modified in some expression to make them suitable for singing in church. Surely this may easily have happened in the instances before us without any corruption or carelessness at all.

Again, in the other pair of parallels, Ps. xiv. and liii., we have an earlier and later edition of the same hymn. What was to prevent the author from improving his poem or slightly altering an expression to make it more suitable for the purpose for which it was afterwards used? Such is a very common case. Only recently the magazines have been dealing with some manuscript copies of Lord Tennyson's poems which tell a curious story as to the many little variations which the author had made between the first writing of them and their appearance in print. Why should not David or Solomon, or any other inspired writer, take as much trouble as Lord Tennyson about a manuscript poem, especially with the solemn feeling that he was writing for the worship of the Temple of God.

And similarly may be explained, perhaps, many of the discrepancies in the other passages referred to. The reader will see that they are cases where the author or compiler of a book transfers bodily into his text a previous composition, either his own or another's, as it suits his purpose. Now, in such a case he is not necessarily bound to adhere strictly to the letter of the borrowed passage. The author of the Book of Kings, for example, transfers a long passage out of Isaiah's writings, and in so doing varies it to suit his purpose, making the history more minute and circumstantial. There is no reason why he should not, just as in the Psalter there is no reason why the compiler of a hymn-book or the original writer of a hymn should not insert or omit verses or slightly alter an expression unsuitable to the occasion for which the hymn was afterwards used. This should cause no difficulty to us. There is much in the Bible of compiling and editing of older writings, which surely was as much under God's guidance as were the original writings themselves. The inspired writers had as much freedom as any other writers in expressing the same thing differently at different times or in adapting the words of earlier documents to suit their present purposes.

Therefore we are not to assume that any two of these similar passages must necessarily have agreed originally word for word. In some cases the changes seem clearly designed. At the same time, there can be little doubt that many of the smaller verbal variations detected by this comparison of passages are the result of inaccuracy on the part of some transcriber.

Let us take one example for illustration from each of our specimens :—

(1.) 2 Sam. xxii. 11, "He *was seen* upon the wings of the wind" is rendered in the parallel, Ps. xviii. 10, "He *did fly* upon the wings of the wind." It might seem at first sight probable that this was an intentional change originally made. But when it is pointed out that the Hebrew words are in the one case וירא ("He was seen"), and in the other וידא ("He did fly"), no unbiassed reader can avoid suspecting a copyist's slip between that old pair of eternal mischief-makers ר and ד (*r* and *d*).[1]

---

[1] These letters closely resembled each other both in the earlier and later alphabets, so this error *may* belong to later times. It is not easy to give an example of copyist's error from similar letters that we can with certainty assign to the Early Ages. Probably we shall find one by comparing 2 Chron. xxii. 1, 2, giving forty-two years as the age of Ahaziah at his accession, with the parallel passage 2 Kings viii. 26,

(2.) Ps. xiv. 2, " The LORD (*Hebrew*, JEHOVAH) looked down from heaven upon the children of men," &c., is rendered in the parallel, Ps. liii. 2, " *God* looked down from heaven," &c.

This is a different class of variation altogether. It points to a time early in Jewish history, when the "unspeakable name" JEHOVAH began to be regarded with such extreme reverence that there was the greatest reluctance to pronounce it, even in reading the Bible. So strong did this feeling become at one period, that it was publicly declared that, " Whosoever uttereth the Sacred Name shall have no part in the world to come." Therefore various expedients were devised. When they met the word they read instead of it " THE NAME," or " GOD," or " ADONAI." We shall hear more of this afterwards in the notes of the Massoretes.

Here is evidently a case where, in making copies of the Psalm for the Temple-singers, the word GOD was not merely *read*, but actually substituted in the manuscript for JEHOVAH; and it is done, the reader will see, everywhere that it occurs throughout this Psalm. Clearly Ps. xiv. is the original poem, and the other is a later copy of it. It is well for the reader, however,

which makes him only twenty-two. Similarity of letters might easily cause this discrepancy, as the Jews, like ourselves, used letters to express numbers, and the ancient letters for twenty and forty might easily be mistaken one for the other. This may perhaps be the source of error also in other very improbable numbers, such as the 50,070 men of the little village of Bethshemesh (1 Sam. vi. 19), slain for irreverence toward the Ark of God, which, if it be an error, must belong to these Early Ages, since it is copied in the Septuagint version of the following period.

to remember that this rare case of a copyist actually altering a word intentionally proceeds, not from carelessness or controversial bias, but from the uttermost extreme of reverence, and therefore gives no grounds for suspicion of inaccurate copying in general. Even this could only have occurred in early times. A later copyist would cut off his right hand rather than make even such a trifling alteration.

VII.

The Verdict.

Space will not permit of our entering more fully here into this subject, or pointing out the passages in which a copyist's error may probably exist.[1] The revisers' margin may be investigated for some "various readings" which they mention with approval, especially in the historical books from Samuel to Chronicles. With others we shall have to deal in the latter part of this book. We are at present inquiring only as to the condition of the text in its earliest period. The evidence, it will be seen, is quite insufficient for any positive decision on the matter; but we are warranted at least in saying that there is reason to believe that all the copies of that period did not correspond minutely in every little word and letter. Besides the considera-

---

[1] For example, that Saul was one year old when he began to reign (see p. 193) ; the mistake about the name Vashni among the sons of Samuel (1 Chron. vi. 28 ; see specimen, p. 202) ; the defect in the verse, "They pierced my hands and my feet" (Ps. xxii. 16), where the Hebrew manuscripts make no sense at all (see specimen, p. 204).

tions already presented there is this also to be taken
into account.   Scholars are all agreed that some
superficial flaws exist in the Hebrew Bible of to-day.
If so, this early period must have had at least its full
share in producing them, partly because some of them
are repeated by the Septuagint version in the following period, and therefore must belong to an earlier
date, partly because the continually increasing care
in the guardianship of the text made their occurrence
less probable after the days of Ezra.

CHAPTER VI.

THE MEN OF THE GREAT SYNAGOGUE.

I.

The Exiles' Return.

The **second period** in the "Story of the Manu-scripts" extends from the time of Ezra to that of our Lord, or more accurately perhaps to the destruction of Jerusalem, A.D. 70.

It is introduced by the touching scene in the eighth chapter of Nehemiah, the thousands of re-turned exiles that September morning bowing in worship in the "broad place that was before the Water Gate" in Jerusalem, and Ezra the scribe, from the pulpit of wood, reading to them out of his Hebrew manuscript the almost forgotten words of Moses. But the glory is departed of the ancient days; the holy tongue sounds strangely in ears accustomed so long to the speech of their Chaldean masters — did this feeling help to cause that sobbing through the crowd ?—for we are told that the Scribes had to give the sense with an interpretation so that the people

might understand the reading. This is an important
fact in the history of the text. From this time forth
the classic Hebrew of the Bible became almost exclu-
sively the property of the educated. The Jews forgot their ancient language for the kindred Aramaic
of business life, just as the Scotch Highlanders and
the Irish to-day are forgetting their poetical mother-
tongue for the more useful English.

A few weeks afterwards there is another solemn
gathering, "when the children of Israel being assembled with fasting and sackcloth and earth upon
them, separated themselves from all strangers, and
stood and confessed their sins and the iniquity of
their fathers." Who can read unmoved their pathetic
pleading? "Thou art a gracious and a merciful
God. Now therefore, our God, the great, the mighty
and terrible God, let not all the trouble seem little
before Thee that hath come upon us since the time
of the kings of Assyria to this day. Howbeit Thou
art just in all that is brought upon us, for Thou hast
done right, but we have done wickedly." [1] And at
last, at the close of their pleading, comes that simple,
beautiful ceremony so expressive of their genuine
repentance and resolve—what an inspiration for a
powerful picture!—the rough roll of skin produced
before the people inscribed with a solemn covenant of
service to Jehovah, the leaders standing forth in their
order; first the priests, then the Levites, then the

[1] Neb. ix. 32; x. 27.

chieftains of the tribes, one by one signing it in Israel's name—

Nehemiah, the Tirshatha, son of Hachaliah; Zede-kiah; Seraiah; Azariah; Jeremiah; Pashur;

and so on through the long roll. It is a scene worth dwelling upon. Fourscore and four men solemnly binding upon themselves and the people for whom they signed "to do justly and love mercy, and walk humbly with their God"—the Church of the Restoration unconsciously fitting itself for the hero-days of the Maccabees. The true glory of Israel was surely not past while such things were still possible in the land.

II.

The Legend of the Great Synagogue.

That list of names, says Jewish tradition, is the first muster-roll of the " men of the Great Synagogue," the men chosen as God's instruments for selecting and revising and preserving for the world the books of the Hebrew Bible. The tradition at least expresses a perception of the fitness of such men for this lofty work. For it was as true then as it was in the days of the Wycliffe Bible in England, that he who meddleth in such studies " hath nede to live a clene life and be full devout in preiers that the Holy Spirit author of wisdom and cunnynge dresse him for his work and suffer him not to err."

According to the Jews, Ezra was president of the Great Synagogue, and at different periods Daniel, Haggai, Zechariah, Malachi, Zerubbabel, Nehemiah, &c., were members. It ceased, they say, at the death of Simon the Just, the last of its members, about the year 300 B.C.

Round this assembly tradition clusters everything important connected with the Jewish Bible. With them ended the voices of the prophets. By them the separate books were revised and edited and formed into a Bible, so that nothing written after them would be received as inspired. By their wisdom the pronunciation was authoritatively fixed, and careful rules for writing and interpretations were made to safeguard the accuracy of the inspired Word. The authorship of Chronicles, Ezra, Nehemiah, and the minor prophets; the change from the ancient Hebrew to the present square writing; the beginning of the celebrated notes of the Massorah; the foundation of colleges for Biblical study, and many things besides, with much or little foundation, the Jews delight to associate with the name of Ezra and his famous Great Synagogue.

• Here is an extract from Rabbi Jacob ben Chajim's well-known introduction to the Rabbinical Bible: " And the men of the Great Synagogue, in whom was heavenly light and powerful like the purest gold, on whose hearts every study of the Law was engraved, have set up marks, and built walls and bars and gates to preserve the citadel in its splendour and brightness. They came to the transparent cloud of its burning doctrine; they sanctified themselves to take the fire from off the altar, so that no other hand might touch and desecrate it. And the Spirit alighted upon them as if by prophecy; they wrote down their labours in books, to which nothing is to be added; and when they had finished their work, the supernatural vision and its sources were sealed, the glory and splendour departed, and the angel of the Lord appeared no more. For no one arose after them who could do as they did. And now we are here this day gathering the gleanings; we capture the faint ones of their rear-guard; we run in their path day and night, and toil, but can never come up to them."

III.

Is the Legend True?

How much of this old Jewish tradition is trust-worthy it is very difficult to say. The Jews assert that the story of the Great Synagogue is as certain as almost any fact in their history; while, on the other hand, some modern critics regard it as little better than a myth founded on the list of names in the Book of Nehemiah.

There is not sufficient evidence for any positive opinion as to the details of the subject. The main facts, however, are beyond all reasonable doubt. We know that there was gathered round Ezra a circle of " men of understanding " (Ezra viii. 16), with whom

E

he took counsel, and who helped him in his work, some of whose names, too, are identical with those of the "signers of the Roll."

We know also that, from that morning at the Water Gate, when the "Great Scribe" stood with his manuscript on the pulpit of wood, there never ceased in Israel a regularly appointed Guild of Scribes. They were the men whose business it was to copy and preserve and expound to the people the ancient oracles of God. They were the men also, a few centuries later, who pursued to the death the Son of God Himself.

Somewhere in this period, too, must be placed the collecting of the scattered Holy Books into a complete Jewish Bible, when the Canon of the Old Testament was closed; so that no books written afterwards would be received as inspired. Whether this was done gradually or at some one solemn council, whether it was done by the traditional "Great Synagogue" or no, are details that may very well be left open to question.[1]

That the change to the later square writing took place then is also positively certain. I do not see why the Jews should not be right that it at least

---

[1] There is a tradition probable enough, 2 Maccabees ii. 13, of the library or collection that Nehemiah made, which, with other books, contained the books about the Kings and Prophets, and the "Writings of David." Thus may have begun the collection of the second part of the Bible. The Pentateuch, of course, is not included in the list. It was from its beginning *par excellence* "*The* Bible," reverenced by the Jews and Samaritans alike. The latter reject all the rest of the Scriptures.

began in the lifetime of Ezra. What more probable than that the copy of the Law which he brought back from Babylon should have been written in the new square characters which during the days of their exile had become so much more familiar to him and to his fellows than the ancient handwriting of their forefathers. At any rate there is positive evidence that some of the manuscripts were thus written not very long after Ezra's time. For on examining the Septuagint (Greek Bible), translated during this period, we discover several mistakes arising from this confusion between similar letters, referred to already ; and we find in many cases that the letters thus confused, while similar in the new square alphabet, had no likeness at all in the ancient writing, and so could not in it have been mistaken the one for the other.

That Ezra and the Great Synagogue so examined and corrected the books of the Old Testament as to leave them absolutely perfect has sometimes been asserted in a past generation even by eminent Hebrew scholars, but there is no good reason to believe anything of the kind. They probably did all that earnest scholarly men could do to correct copyists' errors. They had every facility for so doing ; in many cases very likely the original autograph manuscripts of the inspired writers were before them. But this is the utmost that can be said. That the whole Old Testament together was at any period absolutely word for word as it left the hands of the writers no one who understands its history will venture to say.

IV.

Ancient Criticism—Esau's Teeth.

But traces are not wanting in their day of the beginning of a critical study of the text. They introduced into their manuscripts the two "vowel letters," as they are called, w and y (ו and י), to represent the two principal sounds, and thus to give more definiteness to the consonant-writing.[1]

They attempted, too, a crude sort of Biblical criticism, such as the marking in a certain way words about which there was something peculiar. The reader, perhaps, will wonder how this can be known when no one even of our most ancient writers has ever seen one of these vanished copies. He will find, however, in the following period of the history, that the copyists there make notes about certain dots and marks which had been transferred into their manuscripts from earlier times, and which were so ancient that their meaning had even then become completely lost.

Some of their guesses at the meaning are rather amusing. For instance, in the account of Esau's meeting with Jacob, we are told (Gen. xxxiii. 4) that he fell on his neck and kissed him, and the words "and kissed him" are marked thus by these mysterious dots, which remain to this day in our Hebrew Bibles.

[1] There is no need of perplexing the reader with minute explanations about these vowel letters. They must not be confused with the vowel *points* mentioned already (p. 7, &c.), which did not appear for one thousand years afterwards. But they were the first step in that direction towards defining and fixing the true pronunciation.

Some of the old commentators were greatly exercised in mind about the explanation of this. One thought they denoted that the kiss was sincere; another that it was not sincere; while a third wise teacher sagely informed his readers that these dots were intended to represent the marks of Esau's teeth, and to denote that Esau, in pretending to kiss Jacob, really bit him! I have somewhere met with an extraordinary inquiry into Jacob's kissing Rachel, and why he lifted up his voice and wept, but I do not think it much exceeds in absurdity this wise sage's disquisition about Esau's kissing Jacob.

Stupid as it is, however, it is useful in pointing out the antiquity of these critical remarks. Probably they belonged to somewhere in this second period, and were intended to denote some peculiarity about the words, perhaps the Scribe's doubt as to their correctness. Professor Abbott tells us, in the *Church Quarterly* for April 1889, that one ancient Jewish authority attributes the marks to Ezra himself (not that that counts for anything), and that he gives the curious reason for them that Ezra, not being quite sure whether the words were correct or not, dotted them, so as to save himself from blame in either case—a sort of schoolboy trick, the imputation of which is scarcely very flattering to the " Great Scribe of the Law." " When Ezra," says he, " was asked why he dotted a certain word, he replied, ' When Elijah comes, if he asks why I wrote down that word I will answer, " I have already dotted it " (*i.e.*, as incorrect); but if he asks me why I dotted that word, since it was correct, then I will rub out the dots! ' "

V.

A Famous Witness to the Great Synagogue Bible.

Now comes a very interesting question—Are the Hebrew manuscripts which have come down to us absolutely word for word the same as those which were thus studied and criticised by the Scribes in the ancient Great Synagogue days?   In the absence of all the ancient manu-scripts, is there any pos-sibility of answering this question ?

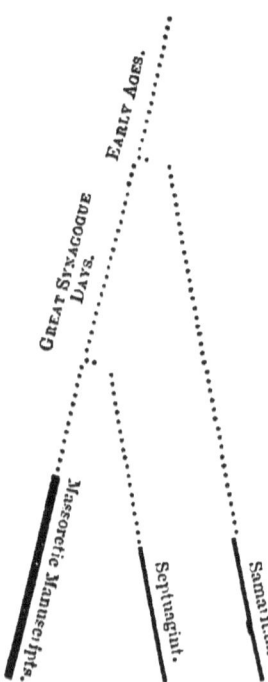

Well, there is a witness to be produced here too, as in the earlier period. The stream has, as it were, been tapped again lower down and a sample taken which if it had been kept pure would have been of incalculable value to-day in determining for us the condition of the ancient Bible.

I refer to the " Sep-tuagint," the Greek ver-sion of the Old Testament, which was begun about 280 years before Christ for the use of the Greek speaking "Jews of the Dispersion,"[1] and was the Bible chiefly used by our Lord and His apostles. It must, of course, have been translated from Hebrew manuscripts of this period.

The strange story of this Septuagint is fully given in Book ii.; therefore we shall refer to it here merely in so far as is necessary for our purpose of using it as a witness.

The first thing that is revealed to us by a close examination is that it agrees *substantially* right through with our present Hebrew Bible, though differing from it sometimes in minor details. Therefore, as we saw in the case of the Samaritan Pentateuch at an earlier date, this Septuagint is a most valuable witness to the fact that our Hebrew Bible of to-day is substantially the same book that was in use three hundred years before Christ.

Now, this is a most important piece of evidence in these sceptical days, and with all the defects of the Samaritan and Septuagint, one must deeply regret the foolish zeal of certain well-meaning writers who, because these documents do not corroborate our Hebrew Bible in every word, try all they can to discredit them as mere corruptions of the Word of God which scarce deserve to be mentioned at all in the investigation of the ancient text. In the first place, this is not true, and if it were true it would be a very bad thing for the Bible. For suppose it should be objected that the Old Testament was a forgery of the

[1] Jas. i. 1 ; 1 Pet. i. 1 (Revised Version).

Scribes shortly before the time of Christ, or that the Jews had seriously tampered with the original deposit on account of the support it gave to the hated Christianity, what a source of doubt and disturbance these charges might become in the absence of all ancient Hebrew manuscripts if God had not preserved for us such providential proofs of the existence of the Bible in those far-back ages, and of its all but complete agreement with the Bible of to-day !

Let me, therefore, again call special attention to the fact that the Pentateuch of the Samaritans proves the substantial agreement of our Pentateuch with that five hundred years before Christ, and that the Septuagint does the same for the whole Old Testament a couple of centuries later.

But in minor details the existing copies of the Septuagint do not always exactly correspond with our Hebrew Bible of to-day. In Jeremiah and Daniel, and also in the historical books, there are many discrepancies, some very trifling, some more important; and also in other books in a lesser degree. A fair illustration of the average amount of variation may be had by comparison of the Bible and Prayer-book versions of the Psalms. The Bible is, of course, translated from the Hebrew, but the Prayer-book version is descended from the unrevised Septuagint, and has many minor variations, and even one rather serious one—the addition to the 14th Psalm of several verses which have no right at all to be there, and which do not exist in the best copies of the Septuagint.

In the Pentateuch, the Septuagint and our Hebrew Bible are almost entirely the same. It is a significant fact as to the purity of transmission of the Pentateuch that, while in the late revision the margin of 1 Samuel alone contains thirty references to Septuagint variations, that of the whole Pentateuch together contains only four!

Now, what are we to say as to these discrepancies in the Septuagint version? Are we to discredit them, as we have done in the case of our former witness, the Samaritan Bible, or must they be received as proof that the manuscripts of Great Synagogue days did not exactly correspond with ours?

Well, some of these discrepancies clearly arise from mistakes in the Septuagint itself. At its best it was not a very accurate version of the Palestine Bible, as the reader will see for himself later on; and to make matters worse, its existing copies have become greatly corrupted in the course of ages.

Nevertheless, after all allowance for the faults of the Septuagint, there are certain of its variations from our Hebrew Bible which it is evident to any scholarly critic must be traced back to the Hebrew manuscripts which lay before its translators as they wrote two thousand years ago—variations, for example, for which we cannot imagine any other possible explanation, or variations which are confirmed by other ancient versions independent of the Septuagint. These must have originated in the Hebrew manuscripts before them.

True, these manuscripts before them were very likely not at all as accurate as those of the Palestine Jews, and this fact must be allowed for in weighing their evidence.

Not to obscure the subject by over-minuteness of explanation, let it suffice here to state the belief among scholars generally as the result of this comparison with the Septuagint Bible, that while the "Great Synagogue" manuscripts were in close substantial agreement with our own, yet they were not *absolutely word for word* uniform with ours, or even with each other. There are plain traces of the existence of variations, though of a trivial and superficial kind.

VI.

The "Abomination of Desolation."

B.C. 168. An awful interruption in the work of the Scribes! A tremendous crisis in the history of the Jewish Bible!

"O God, the heathen are come into Thine inheritance; Thy holy Temple have they defiled, and made Jerusalem an heap of stones! The dead bodies of Thy servants have they given to be meat unto the fowls of the air, and the flesh of Thy saints unto the beasts of the land. Their blood have they shed like water on every side of Jerusalem, and there was no man to bury them!" [1]

How should I tell in a passing paragraph that story

---

[1] Ps. lxxix., most probably written at this period.

of the Maccabean days, curdling one's very blood with
horror, while yet making every nerve thrill high with
the fierce excitement of battle and revenge! In the
pages of Josephus, in the Books of the Maccabees,
find the story, and study it for yourself, my reader—
the invasion of Antiochus, the mad Syrian king; the
raid not chiefly against city and people, but against
God and religion and the holy manuscripts, the most
sacred treasure of the Jewish race.

Read of the patriots turning at bay, of the town
and Temple walls bespattered with blood, of Bibles
torn asunder and burned in the fire, of the fierce rage
of men, of the wailing of women, of the great sow
slaughtered in insult in the Temple itself, and the
broth of its filthy flesh sprinkled, amid shouts of
laughter, on the sacred parchments![1]

Look to the heights at the battle of Emmaus,
where fierce Judas the Maccabee prepares for revenge; see the mourners in sackcloth calling upon
God, spreading out in the sunlight before Him the
charred and torn fragments of their holy books,
defiled by touch of the accursed Greeks, and painted all
over in wanton insult with the obscene figures of their
heathen gods.[2] Ay, and though it does not concern
this history, look a little longer still; hear the fierce
trumpet-blast of Israel's host; see the stern warriors
sweeping down from the hills crying for vengeance to
the God of Sabaoth.——Enough of the wild story.

[1] Josephus, Antiquities, xii. 5. 4; Diod. Sic., xxxiv. 1.
[2] 1 Maccabees iii. 46-50.

Full well that day did they avenge their wrongs, when the blood of a thousand of the Syrian host atoned for the swine-broth sprinkled on the Bible.

What would the world do, men ask, if it lost the Bible? Did you ever think, did you ever know, reader, how nearly, humanly speaking, the world had lost it—the Old Testament at least, and all of the New which was quarried from the old? The destruction of a few parchments flung into the fire meant very little for the Syrian soldiers; for us it went perilously nigh to mean the Hebrew Bible swept away for ever!

Nor was the danger over then. Solemnly, lovingly, as the relics of the dead, were these sacred remnants cherished by the nation, and new fair copies soon replaced the old, copies perhaps honoured by the touch of Christ. And then—another scene of horror, another time of peril to the holy books, and Jerusalem was captured, and the Temple lay in ruins, and in the pile of the proud Romans' trophies lay the Temple manuscript of the Books of Moses.[1]

And yet again, a half-century later, in the final struggle of the Jews at Bethur, when Scribes and manuscripts together were flung in hundreds into the raging flames. Surely a higher than human care was guarding that old Hebrew Bible!

[1] Josephus, Jewish Wars, vii. 5. 5.

CHAPTER VII.

THE TALMUD PERIOD.

I.

The College of Tiberias.

With the destruction of Jerusalem begins a new era in the " Story of the Hebrew Manuscripts." The State was broken up ; the Temple was in ruins ; it seemed as if all now might well be at an end. But no. From the moment that their national life died out at the destruction of the holy city, the Jews, with nothing left to live for in the present, threw themselves heart and soul into the preservation of the relics of their glorious past. The sacred writings were everything to them—their title-deeds, their national records, their covenant with Jehovah. And so upon the sacred writings their attention was centred with an earnestness such as never had been known before. Religion and patriotism united to inspire their reverence. Every word, every letter, became holy in their eyes.

Quickly the centres of learning grew for the study of the Hebrew Scriptures. At Japhneh, at Lydda,

at Cæsarea, famous academies arose where grammar
and criticism and interpretation were taught. But
famous above all were the schools of Tiberias looking
out on the waters of the sacred lake. Travellers who
now visit the decaying little town remind us of the
glory of its ancient days—of turret and dome and
sculptured figure—of Herod's golden palace flashing
in the sun. Seldom do we hear of the greater glory,
when Herod and his golden palace were forgotten,
when earnest students paced its terraced paths in high
communings with the sages of their people, when
its archives were the treasuries of Biblical lore, and
the fame of its great schools was spread throughout
the Jewish world.

It was the last retreat of old Judaism in Palestine
before the advancing wave of Christianity. The Jewish
element reigned supreme. Not heathen or Samaritan
or dog of a Christian could find a resting-place within
its walls. It was the great university of the Hebrew
world, and many a glorious name figured on its roll.
Rabbi Judah the Holy was one of its teachers, and
Rabbi Johanan of Talmud fame, Aquila and Symmachus, the great Bible translators,[1] were pupils in its
halls of the Rabbi Akiba, whose life-story forms one
of the most romantic chapters in the whole of the
Hebrew literature. And even when its golden days
were over, when, retreating before the spread of Christianity, it had sent forth its greatest students into
other lands, the glory of the old academy lived again

[1] See Book ii. p. 158.

in the glory of her children, and Tiberias was almost eclipsed by the Babylon schools on the banks of the far Euphrates.

II.

The Makers of the Talmud.

In almost every Jewish academy the whole course of study was connected with the Scriptures, especially with the Mosaic books. When Rabbi Ishmael was asked at what time the "Greek wisdom" might be studied, "At some hour," said he, "which is neither day nor night, for it is written concerning the Book of the Law, 'Day and night thou shalt meditate therein'" (Joshua i. 8).

It was not altogether, though, such a study as we should approve of. Much attention was given to the traditional explanations of the Torah or Law of Moses, and the systematic collection of these traditions into what was called the MISHNA. In course of time, fearing lest this oral Mishna should become lost or corrupted, it was committed to writing, chiefly under the care of Rabbi Judah and his *confrères* in the College of Tiberias. And then there grew to it a series of commentaries or "Gemaras," both in Palestine and Babylon, till at length these increasing "traditions of men" about the Scriptures threatened to bury altogether the Scriptures themselves. The Mishna, together with its Gemara or commentary, made up what is called THE TALMUD. And by degrees this Talmud grew to be

to them more important than the Scriptures themselves. "He that is learned in the Scriptures," said
they, "and not in the Mishna, is a blockhead. The
Law was given to Moses by day, the Mishna by
night. The Law is like salt, the Mishna like pepper,
the Gemara like balmy spice." And thus their devotion to the Talmud became the very curse of Judaism.
Professing to be the hedge and safeguard of the
Scriptures, it was really "making void the Word of
God by its tradition, teaching for doctrines the commandments of men."

III.

Their " Biblical Criticism."

Fault-finding, however, is an ungracious task, especially with men tó whom we owe so much as we do to
the Talmud Scribes. The making of the Talmud—
we shall hear more of it hereafter—was but part of
their work. For the other part—their critical care of
the Hebrew text—the world cannot be too thankful.

It is not easy to define exactly what they accomplished, for the work, as we have seen, was begun by
the Scribes, in the period before them, and finished
long afterwards in the days of the Massorets. They
did not attempt anything like a regular revision.
They marked certain readings that seemed to them
doubtful. If they met with a clear mistake they corrected it in the margin, but seldom or never meddled
with the text. They gave minute directions about

copying of manuscripts and cautions about such errors
as similar letters. They counted the number of verses
and words in each book in order to preserve it from
future corruption. They recorded, but in a rambling,
unmethodical way, the textual notes of their predecessors for centuries before.

The Talmud contains many traces of their rough-
and-ready method of Biblical criticism. It enumerates
certain words which they found in their Bible manuscripts with a little mark already placed over them,
thus showing us that at least some rude sort of textual
criticism existed even before their days. These same
words may be seen in our Hebrew Bible to-day with
this mark above them, supposed by some to be the
"tittle" referred to by our Lord, and probably indicating originally words that were omitted in some
manuscripts.

Their simple method of choosing between two varying readings in different manuscripts would certainly
not satisfy our revisers of the Jerusalem Chamber,
with their perfect critical apparatus beside them.
There is a Talmud note, for instance, on Deut. xxxiii.
27 where the manuscripts disagreed as to a certain
word. "Rabbi Simeon-ben-Lakish said that three
copies were found in the hall of the Temple. In one
of them they found written מעוני (MEONI), in two of
them מעונה (MEONAH), and they adopted, therefore,
the text of the two against that of the one."

It was certainly a very mechanical mode, and one
that might easily have often set them wrong, for in

F

manuscripts, as in men, truth is by no means always with the majority. But it was the best way they knew. And, all things considered, we may be thankful for their hard and fast rule of deciding by majority instead of arbitrarily choosing, with their fanciful and unscientific minds, what might seem to them the best readings. Anyhow, the fact that they shrank from introducing any changes into the text, and merely kept them in the margin—for a long time, indeed, only in their memories—does much to secure the text even when they decided on the wrong word.

But the great security of the text amongst the Talmudists is the extreme reverence and awe with which it was regarded. Human nature is a strange compound. The very men who practically were putting their commentary in the place of the Bible almost worshipped the letter of that Bible itself. They wrote every word in it with scrupulous care; they washed their pens before the Holy Name; they dared not alter even a plain mistake except by a correction in the margin of the text. " My son," said Rabbi Ishmael, " take great heed how thou doest thy work, for thy work is the work of Heaven, lest thou drop or add a letter of the manuscript, and so become a destroyer of the world." Never were saintly relics reverenced as were these old manuscripts. Never was a book so marvellously guarded. Nothing, surely, but the conviction that " to them were committed the oracles of God " could account for such a jealous care.[1]

---

[1] We have little conception of the awe and reverence of the Jews

IV.

The Bible of the Academies.

Now, what was the condition of this carefully-guarded Bible of the academies in the early Christian centuries as compared with that of our present Massoretic manuscripts? Though there are no Hebrew manuscripts of this period remaining, yet by means of Greek and other translations we can investigate the text up almost to the days of our Lord. There are three celebrated Greek versions—those of Aquila, Symmachus, and Theodotion, made before the year 200 A.D.[1] The first two of these writers are said to have been students in the College of Tiberias, and therefore would be witnesses of the most approved Palestine text. Now, a scholar can easily turn these translations back into their original Hebrew, and then they are found to agree, not exactly, but very closely, with the existing manuscripts—much more closely than the Septuagint version or the Pentateuch of the Samaritans.

The Syriac (Peshitto) version of the second century is also clearly founded on Hebrew manuscripts like ours,

to this day for the words of the holy tongue. Even if it be not Scripture, merely a leaf of the Hebrew Prayer-book which has got torn or has fallen on the floor, it is touched with a superstitious awe, as an idolator would touch his idol. To be sure, with the lower classes it is more superstition than any real feeling of religion. The writer was told by an eye-witness the other day of a Jewish boy treading inadvertently on such a page, and receiving from his horrified father a blow that almost felled him to the ground.

[1] For an account of these Versions see Book ii. p. 158.

and the Targums (*i.e.*, translations into the common
vernacular of the Jews) seem to have precisely the
same text underlying them.

About A.D. 230 we have the testimony of Origen,
the best scholar of his age, who undertook to compare
in parallel columns the Hebrew with the Septuagint,
and the three other Greek versions just mentioned.
His evidence is to the same effect, with this addition,
that the Hebrew manuscripts of his day seem to have
been almost uniform in text. He seems never to
think of any variations, but to have before him a
standard Hebrew text, with which he labours to bring
the versions into agreement.

As we come down towards the year 400, the existence of the present Massoretic text is perfectly clear.
St. Jerome, the only Hebrew scholar of his day in
the Western Church, made his famous Vulgate version
from manuscripts almost exactly the same as ours. He
points out certain errors in the Septuagint which he
says " do not agree with the Hebrew," and quotes the
Hebrew exactly as it is now. He also, curiously
enough, writes out certain Hebrew verses in ordinary
Roman letters, showing us not only that he had it in
the passages quoted word for word as we have, but
also that he pronounced the words with the same
vowels as ours, though there were no vowel points in
existence in his time. Of course, they were Palestine
manuscripts that he used. His teachers were all
scribes from the Palestine schools. He tells us of
one who used to come by night to him, like Nicodemus,

"secretly for fear of the Jews;" and in his preface to the Books of Chronicles he mentions a doctor from the College of Tiberias, in high esteem among the Hebrews, as his principal instructor and helper in the work.[1]

v.

The "Palestine Text."

We trace, then, back to the days of our Lord a Hebrew text almost exactly the same as that which has come down to us in the Massoretic manuscripts. We have seen, too, that, from the care bestowed on it before that time, we are justified in believing that, with some slight variations, it is the identical text of the " Great Synagogue" days, when many of the authors of the later books were alive. Though there is but little material for our history in the still earlier period, all the evidence goes to show the marvellously correct transmission of the Mosaic writings; and whatever variations existed in the manuscripts of the later books, we have every reason to believe were corrected as far as possible in the Great Synagogue days, when the separate books were collected into a " Bible."

The reader will keep in mind that we are dealing with the text *as used by the Palestine Jews.* The

---

[1] One of his teachers was the Rabbi Barrabanus, whose name, as a great stroke of wit, was shortened into Barrabas by one of Jerome's assail-ants. He is abusing Jerome for finding errors in the Septuagint, and triumphantly demands, " Which are most likely to be right, the seventy translators guided by the Holy Ghost, or the one translator guided by Barrabas?" Humour was not a strong point with these old fathers.

Samaritan Pentateuch and the (Greek) Septuagint represent long-lost manuscripts, differing more or less from this. They form a very interesting study, and in some instances, as we shall see, suggest the true readings in cases where the received text is faulty. But we cannot depend on them. Our chief reason for believing in the superior accuracy of the existing Hebrew Scriptures is, that they contain the Palestine text, which has been for all these ages in the hands of scholarly priests and scribes, and guarded with the most scrupulous care. The manuscripts used for the Septuagint were in the hands of men who, as far as we can judge, had neither the same Hebrew scholarship, the same frightened awe about the letter of the text, nor the same strict notions of a copyist's work which obtained amongst the Palestine Jews. In Alexandria especially, the home of the Septuagint, the tendency was towards a much freer dealing with Scripture than the rigid formal literalism of the Jews of Palestine would allow. The sense, not the very words and letters, was the chief consideration, and they would probably not hesitate to slightly expand or alter the form of an expression, if thus they could express the sense more clearly.

Now, it is evident that this tone of mind, healthy as it is in a student or expositor, is by no means conducive to an accurate preserving and transmitting of the text. The Palestine temper was the very opposite. Be it narrowness and superstition, be it worship of the letter while neglecting the spirit, be it foolish mysticism about the meaning of trifles, be it what it may, the fear and reverence engendered for every jot and tittle of the sacred writings has been, in God's providence, a most marvellous safeguard in the correct transmission of the Old Testament in Palestine.

CHAPTER VIII.

THE STORY OF THE MANUSCRIPTS.

THE DAYS OF THE MASSORETES.

I.

Who were the Massoretes?

After the completion of the Talmud in the fifth century the academies were freer than ever for the study of the sacred text. We have seen that in the previous periods a number of oral traditions had been gradually accumulating respecting the right method of reading the text, the accuracy of certain passages, &c. These had grown to a considerable body of notes at the close of the Talmud period, but were preserved only in a confused way in the traditions of various academies, and in the memories of various Rabbis. But as the circumstances of their national life made it increasingly difficult to preserve these oral traditions, it now became desirable to collect them into some order and commit them to writing, and this was the beginning of the written MASSORAH, so famous in the history of the Hebrew text. It will be remembered that for ages all these notes and corrections were oral, handed down by tradition through the college's of the Scribes from one generation to another. They were, therefore, always referred to as the MASSORAH, *i.e., the tradition;* the men who collected and committed them to writing are called the MASSORETES, and the text which these scholars have handed down to us certified as in their opinion correct is known as the MASSORETIC TEXT. In the hands of the Massoretic Scribes the original deposit was greatly enlarged and improved. They arranged into a complete commentary the remarks of their predecessors. They examined the manuscripts critically and completely, whereas the Talmudists had but made disconnected notes. They studied the languages, the grammar, the interpretation of the Scriptures. They invented the vowel points and accents to stereotype the correct reading.

Thus slowly and gradually the Massorah [1] grew. It belongs not to any one age or any one set of scholars. It began probably with a few short technical notes to guard against copyists' blunders in places liable to error, and gradually grew during many ages into a commentary on the whole text, a great "critical apparatus" for the amending and preserving of the Old Testament Scriptures.

Therefore, though we apply the term to the men of the period who completed and wrote the Massorah, the Massoretes, in truth, might be said to have existed

---

[1] The reader must keep clearly in mind that the Massorah was not the text itself, but the mass of critical and other notes concerning the text.

almost from the days of Ezra. "Indeed," says Elias
Levita, "there were hundreds and thousands of Massoretes, and they continued, generation after generation,
for very many years."

Dr. Ginsburg, the highest living authority, puts the
beginning of the Massorah about three centuries before
Christ, and it was not completed for 1300 years. What
we have here designated as the "days of the Massoretes," *i.e.*, the period when the Massorah was completed and written out, may be roughly set down at
from 500 to 1000 A.D.

II.

Contents of the Massorah.

A merely general notion of the contents of the
Massorah is all that can be given here. It deals
minutely with the books, sections, verses, words,
letters, vowel points, accents, and such matters. It
gives conjectures, or, where possible, definite corrections, of anything apparently wrong in the text. It
indicates where anything was supposed to have been
added or left out or altered, or whether certain words
were written with or without the vowel letters (see
p. 68). It puts particular marks on words about
which there was anything in the least unusual. It
records the "various readings." It counts up the verses,
the words, even the letters of the separate books, and
invents mnemonic signs by which to remember them

PIECE OF A MASSORETIC MANUSCRIPT IN THE LIBRARY OF TRINITY COLLEGE, DUBLIN, with the Massorah notes below in small Hebrew letters, fancifully written into the form of a—what shall I call him—a reptile? For account of this curious fashion of writing footnotes, see p. 91.

[To face page 91.]

easily. It tells how often the same word occurs at the beginning, middle, or end of a verse. It gives the middle verse, the middle word, the middle letter, of each book of the Law, &c., &c.

But to continue a long enumeration of this kind will probably but confuse the reader. Clearness is more important to aim at than completeness. Therefore it will be best rather to try by means of a few examples in simple form to leave in the reader's mind a distinct, even if a very partial, notion of what the Massorah contains.

III.

Its Two Classes of Notes.

At first the Massorah notes existed only in separate books and sheets, which were used in the public lectures of the Scribes. Afterwards, for convenience' sake, they were transferred to the margin of the Old Testament manuscripts. But this was very clumsily done. The remarks were not always placed on the same page with the verse to which they belonged. The writers had a fashion, too, of making them up into all sorts of fancy shapes, of men and fishes and flowers and birds, as shown in the opposite photograph. If there was too much matter for the figure, they did not hesitate to transfer the overplus to the end of the book; if too little, they calmly inserted bits from other places to fill up the gap. Thus it became a

Herculean task to reduce the Massorah into anything like order.

The notes, for the most part, might be brought under two separate heads referring to :—

(1.) *What* IS *in the text.* An elaborate system of rules and annotations intended to secure the exact transmission of the text before them in the smallest particulars, to preserve from corruption every jot and tittle of the Scriptures.

(2.) *What* SHOULD BE *in the text.* Corrections of mistakes and guesses about doubtful readings, which, however, they did not venture to meddle with in the text itself, but only recorded in the margin of the manuscript.

IV.

What is in the Text.

(1.) As the first illustration of the notes concerning WHAT IS IN THE TEXT, I take an extract from the " Massoreth - Hammassoreth " of Elias Levita, a mediaeval writer on the Massorah, whom I have referred to already—

" The Massoretes by their diligence have learned and marked that the ו in נחון (Lev. xi. 42) is the middle of all the letters of the Pentateuch ; that 'Moses *diligently sought*' (Lev. x. 16) is the middle of all the words ; that 'the breastplate' verse (Lev. viii. 8) is the middle of all the verses. This they have done in

all the sacred books. Moreover, they have counted
the verses, words, and letters of each section in the
Pentateuch, and made marks accordingly. Thus the
section ' Bereshith ' (the first section in Genesis) has
146 verses, the sign is AMAZIAH." He means that the
Hebrew letters having regular numerical values like
our Roman numerals, the Hebrew letters AMAZIAH,
like the Roman letters CXLVI., denote 146, and thus
make a mnemonic for the number of the verses.

(2.) " They have also counted each separate letter
in the Scriptures, and have noted that—

"א (A) occurs 42,377 times.
"ב (B)   „   35,218   „   &c., &c.

" Indeed," continues Levita, " a beautiful poem
was written long ago on this subject, beginning ' The
Tabernacle, the place of my court,' " &c.

Well, it is an ingenious poem anyhow, and a useful
poem for its purpose of enabling one to remember the
number of the letters. As to its beauty, there is no
accounting for tastes. I fear, though, its claim can
only be based on the philosophical principle that " the
useful is the truly beautiful," on which principle we
have an exquisitely beautiful poem in English, beginning—

" Thirty days hath September,
April, June, and November," &c.

Here is the first stanza of this " beautiful poem"

on the letter א (A).   I represent the Hebrew by
English letters :—

"ACHEL MEKON BENYANAI,
SHESHAM HALO ZEKEENAI."

" The Tabernacle is my court,
Whither my elders do resort."

"The whole congregation   " For a sacrifice of peace
together was **forty and two** offering, **two** oxen, **five** rams,
thousand three hundred and **five** he goats, **five** lambs"
threescore " (Neh. vii. 66). (Numb. vii. 17).

Now for the explanation of this "poem."   In the
above Hebrew words the " A." marks the letter discussed, the other initial letters, M., B., SH., H., Z.,
represent numbers whose total value is 42,377, the
number of A's in the Old Testament.   To make assurance doubly sure, the two verses underneath are added
as a further mnemonic : the number of the congregation in one verse (42,360), and the number of
animals in the other (17), when added together, make
the same number, 42,377.   Thus every letter in the
alphabet is laboriously gone through, with the pious
object of preventing the insertion or omission of a
single letter in the deposit committed to them by
God.   I dare say these precautions were not always
effectual.   It would require a high faith in human
nature to believe that every scribe took the trouble
of counting and checking the separate letters in his
manuscript.   Yet it must have been in some degree
a security against errors, and in any case it shows the

care with which the appointed record-keepers of God guarded their sacred charge.

(3.) Again, they would put asterisks, or rather little circles, over certain words in a verse, calling attention to a footnote. If the word occurs only in that place the note says, " None other ; " if more than once, it announces, " three, four, six, &c., times," giving the places where it occurs, something after the style of Cruden's Concordance, only that the old Massoretes had not the convenience of numbered chapters and verses. These were usually words about which a copyist might easily err; for example, under the phrase " The Spirit of GOD " (ELOHIM) the note says " It occurs 8 times," and indicates the places. In all other cases but these eight it is " The Spirit of THE LORD " (JEHOVAH), and the note keeps the copyist from dropping into this easy mistake of writing the more common phrase. They write also such notes as these :—" There are two verses in the Torah (Law) beginning with M: eleven verses in which the first and last letter is N: there are forty verses in which Lo is read three times," &c. They explain that such a verb is connected with such a noun, such a word should be so construed, and so on.

(4.) Here is a curious illustration of another class of notes. I give it to show the marvellous carefulness of these men, and how they considered no detail too minute or insignificant to be attended to in their sacred guardianship of the Word of God.

In Joshua ix. 1 we read: "When all the kings that were on this side Jordan, the Hittite and the Amorite, the Canaanite, the Perizzite, the Hivite, and the Jebusite, heard thereof." Here are six kings mentioned, and the conjunction "and" occurs only twice, before the second and before the sixth. What possible safe-guard can there be to preserve that insignificant little word in its proper position? Would not a copyist, if not especially on his guard, almost inevitably get it into the wrong places?

See how the Massoretes guard against this danger. Underneath this verse about the kings they put, in a footnote, a little catch-word, "THE GOLD FOR THE KINGS," and refer us to a certain section in the Book of Numbers. There we find the word GOLD in Numb. xxxi. 22, which reads as follows: "Only the Gold and the silver, the brass, the iron, the tin, and the lead." Here again we have six nouns, and we find that the conjunction "and" is before the second and sixth. Thus we learn that these are the right positions for the conjunction in the verse from which we have been referred. These two verses are thus a check on each other—a check which, though it seem slight to the English reader, was effective enough for the Hebrew Scribes, with their intimate knowledge of and scrupulous care for every letter of the text. But whatever be the reader's estimate of its value, in any case it illustrates the laborious and accurate care-fulness of the Massoretes.

V.

What should be in the text.

The above are examples of their care to preserve uncorrupt what *is* in the text. But sometimes they had reason to believe that the manuscripts before them had become corrupted already in some places, and this necessitated another set of marginal comments to indicate in their opinion what *should be* in the text, for their reverence for the sacred letters (*i.e.*, the consonants) of the text itself was carried so far that they would not dare to meddle with them, even to correct an obvious mistake. The reader must learn the two Hebrew words continually used in this class of notes :—

קְרִי = Keri = what must be read.

כְּתִיב = Kethibh = what is written.

(1.) Suppose, now, the Massoretes, in making a new copy, found in the manuscript before them a word which they had reason to believe was incorrect. Their superstitious reverence for the text would not allow them to correct it boldly. What then did they do ? They wrote down in their new copy the *consonants* of this incorrect word just as they found them. Then they wrote in the margin the consonants of what they believed to be the correct word, and put *its vowels* under the consonants of the wrong word which they had just transcribed, with an asterisk calling attention to the margin. This incorrect word in the text then with these vowels could not be read without making

G

nonsense, so the reader had to turn to the consonants of the right word in the margin. It was as if we should print in our English Bible :—

Bless the Lord, O my soul, and forget not all His C͜MM͜NDM͜NTS.*   * Read B N F T S.

i.e., "*benefits*" is the word that should be read instead of "commandments." The right word in the margin was called the "Keri" (what should be read). The wrong word in the text was the "Kethibh" (that which is written). There is a good example in Ps. xvi. 10, where the text has "Thy holy ones," while the "Keri" correctly gives the singular in the margin, "Suffer Thine Holy *One* to see corruption." The most frequent example of a "Keri" is the unutterable name JHVH, which, owing to the "Keri," we have learned to mispronounce as Jehovah. No one can tell now with any certainty what are its true vowels; probably it should be read as Yahveh. With such awe was the word regarded that it was forbidden to be uttered by any except the high priest, and by him only once a year in the Holy of Holies.[1] On all other occasions the word

[1] One old legend tells that whenever the high priest pronounced the name it was heard as far as to Jericho, but all the hearers immediately forgot it. Later stories attribute the miracles of Jesus to His utterance of the Sacred Name, the true pronunciation of which He had learned in some mysterious way. But the most curious thing about this old superstition is the way in which its results remain to us still. In consequence of it the Septuagint version always used the word LORD for JHVH, and through the Septuagint the habit has crept not only into the works of the New Testament writers, who all used the Septuagint, but even into our English Old Testament of to-day, often very much spoiling the force and meaning in passages where Jehovah is contrasted with other gods.

Adonai (Lord) was usually directed to be read instead, and to indicate this the vowels of $A_oD_oN_aI$ were put under the letters of the "most holy word," thus $J_oH_oV_aH$.

(2.) One class of the marginal "Keris" was, I should think, rather a danger than a protection to the text, though, at the same time, one could wish that some of them were retained to-day in our English Bibles for reading the Old Testament Lessons in church. They are called euphemistic "Keris." Where a coarse, indecorous expression occurs in the text, the Scribes, while not daring to meddle with the expression itself, put in the margin words that were more fitted for reading in public, and the "Keri" directed that the reader should use them instead of the others.

3. Sometimes a word or phrase is in the text that *should be omitted*—a usual case is where the copyist has carelessly repeated a word. The reader will probably find examples often in his own letter-writing of such redundancy; it is a very common slip of writers. In such a case we should just score out the word. The Massoretes dared not do this, so they left its consonants in the text, but called attention to the error by leaving it without vowels, and writing in the margin, "*Kethibh, not Keri,*" *i.e.*, "Written, but not to be read;"[1] as, for example, Jer. li. 3 : "Against the bender let the archer bend his bow," where the word

[1] The Massorah gives eight instances : Ruth iii. 12 ; 2 Sam. xiii. 33, xv. 21 ; 2 Kings v. 18 ; Jer. xxxviii. 16, xxxix. 12, li. 3 ; Ezek. xlviii. 16.

"bender" has been repeated by a slip of some early copyist, or, for aught we know, of the original writer himself. This is how it appears in the Massoretic manuscripts :—

AG$_{ai}$NST TH$_e$ B$_e$ND$_e$R TH BNDR $*$ * Kethibh, not Keri

L$_e$T TH$_e$ ARCH$_e$R B$_e$ND H$_i$S B$_o$W   (written ; not to be read).

4. The converse of this case occurs very frequently. The context clearly shows that one or more words have been omitted. The Massoretes, of course, would not supply the words, but leave a blank wherein they insert the *vowels* required by the missing word or words, and put the consonants of them in the margin with a note, " Keri, not Kethibh," *i.e.*, " Should be read, though not written." [1]   Take, as an example, 2 Sam. viii. 3 :—

H$_e$ W$_e$NT T$_o$ R$_e$C$_o$V$_e$R H$_i$S B$_o$RD$_e$R   * PHRTS, Keri, not Kethibh

AT TH$_e$ R$_i$V$_e$R $_{eu}$ · · · $_a$ · · · $*$ (to be read, though not written).

i.e., in the opinion of the Massoretes, the word $_{eu}$PHR$_a$TS (Euphrates) should be read after " river."

It may be well to remark here that these notes, while showing the extreme care of the Massoretes, must not always be regarded as infallible. We have to use our judgment and the ancient versions in deciding. Our English Authorised Version follows sometimes the "Keri" (marginal correction), sometimes the "Kethibh" (what is written, in text). The Revised Version seems usually to prefer keeping the " Kethibh " in the text

[1] The Massorah gives ten instances, some of which are questioned in the Revised Version : Judges x. 13 ; Ruth iii. 5, 17 ; 2 Sam. viii. 3, xvi. 23, xviii. 20 ; 2 Kings xix. 31, 37 ; Jer. xxxi. 38, l. 29.

and leaving the " Keri" in the margin, with the note, " Another reading is," [1] &c.

This is one of the great advantages of the Massoretic reverence for the letter of the text. We not only get their opinion in the margin as to the right reading, but we have preserved for us also in the text the old reading, which they rightly or wrongly regarded as incorrect. If they, with their defective knowledge of textual criticism, had ventured to correct the text as they thought best, they would probably have done as much harm as good, and the old, and in many cases true, readings would have been entirely lost.

VI.

The Vowels and Accents.

The invention of the vowel-points is another very important part of the work of the Massoretes. This subject has been already dealt with in an earlier chapter. It is scarcely necessary to add anything further here, except, perhaps, to emphasise the fact that the Massoretic vowel-system did not introduce any change in the old traditional reading, but only fixed and stereotyped it. The Massoretes found certain vowel-sounds supplied in the reading of the consonant text. They merely invented signs to represent these sounds, so that there should be no possibility afterwards of any variation in the reading. These vowel-

---

[1] There are cases, however, such as Ps. c. 3 ; Isa. ix. 3, where the revisers have made a great improvement by substituting the " Keri" of the Massoretes for the "Kethibh," which has been retained in the Authorised Version (see specimen, p. 206).

signs they regarded as a mere human unconsecrated thing, quite external to the holy text itself, and only used for convenience' sake.[1] They never admitted them into the sacred rolls of the Synagogue.

It is, therefore, scarcely necessary to add that we are not bound to accept the Massoretic vowels as infallible. They represent the highest tradition as to the correct reading. They are generally the only possible reading. But we must remember that the original authors of the Bible wrote only the consonants. Therefore, if in any particular place we are able to make sense by reading the vowels differently, it is quite possible that our reading may be right. See, for example, " Jacob's bed " and " Jacob's staff" in page 12.

We owe to them also the Hebrew accents, those curious marks that may be noticed in our specimen (p. 1), dotted about over the text. I despair of arousing my readers' enthusiasm about these accents, mere grammar marks, as they have grown to be to the English reader of Hebrew now, or, at most, signs for recording the true chanting tones of the Synagogue. Only the living voice—only, I think, the Jewish voice can convey any idea of this beautiful contrivance for recording the modulations and inflections of the speaker's tones. They almost placed upon the paper the spoken words. They marked the sense and logical connection. They represented pause, emphasis, emo-

---

[1] The story in Chapter II. of the controversy about the vowel-points in Reformation times refers, of course, to a half-educated body of Jews six hundred years after this period.

tion, whisper, tremulousness—everything that we imperfectly try to denote by italics, and capitals, and dashes, and punctuation marks. Get a refined, educated Jew, an enthusiastic man, capable of flashing eyes and trembling excitement over his subject; let him read for you a touching passage in the Prophets according to these accents by which the Massoretes tried to reproduce the original utterance, and you will—well at least you will probably be very much dissatisfied with the reading of the First Lesson in church the next Sunday.

VII.

Manuscript Copying.

Their rules for copying Synagogue manuscripts will help to emphasise what has been said as to the precautions against transcribers' errors.

They must be transcribed from an ancient and approved manuscript solely with pure black ink made of soot, charcoal, and honey, upon the skin of a "clean" animal prepared expressly for the purpose by a Jew. The sheets or skins are to be fastened together with strings made from the sinews of a clean animal. The scribe must not write a single word from memory; he must attentively look upon each individual word in his exemplar, and orally pronounce it before writing it down. In writing any of the sacred names of God, he must solemnise his mind by devotion and reverence; before writing any of them he must wash his pen; before writing the Ineffable

Name (Jʜᴠʜ) he must wash his whole body. The copy must be examined within thirteen days. Some writers assert that the mistake of a single letter vitiates the entire codex; others assert that it is permitted to correct three in any one sheet; if more are found the copy is to be condemned as profane. Probably many of the Synagogue rolls in Gentile libraries to-day are only these discarded copies.[1]

VIII.

The Last of the Massoretes.

Foremost in the great work of the Massorah was the College of Tiberias, and away on the Euphrates the Babylon schools, now rivalling their ancient mother in repute. The two sets of scholars worked independently of each other, and did not always entirely agree in their result. The points of difference, however, are of very minor importance, and the Western or Palestine school ultimately prevailed, though not to the entire exclusion of the other.

I wish, reader, it were allowed me, in closing this chapter, to write for you the story of " The Last of the Massoretes;" to tell of the Massorah completed; of the academies broken up and rude Arab tribes holding revel in the halls; of outcast Jewish scholars wandering through the land to seek precarious shelter in Germany and Spain. About the year when William the Conqueror was born Aaron ben-Asher was Prin-

---

[1] See Scott Porter, Text Crit., p. 72, note.

cipal of the College of Tiberias, and Jacob ben-
Naphthali of the Babylon schools, and no man was
enrolled after them in the number of the Massorah
Scribes. Two famous Rabbis were they, worthy to
close the long illustrious list of the scholarly " men
of the Massorah." Each of them exerted his powers
to the utmost that his academy should produce an
immaculate copy of the Scriptures, and in such reputation were their manuscripts held that they became the
standards for the Massoretic text.

But history affords no materials for the story. No
historian of their day recognised their importance.
No chronicler was touched by the romantic nobleness
of the task, to picture the last days of the rival
academies and the end of the great work thirteen
centuries long. Silent and signless the Massoretes
disappeared. Let us not forget what we owe to their
labours. Let us not be unmindful of His good hand
upon us who sent them to preserve for us the " Oracles
of God."

IX.

A Mysterious Document

Now that we have gone through the " Story of the
Manuscripts," we cannot help feeling that an important
question still remains unsolved. What was the document from which the Massoretic manuscripts were
copied? No one can look over a number of these
manuscripts, or even examine the printed text of an
ordinary Hebrew Bible, noticing how every peculiarly

shaped letter, every correction, nay, even every little irregularity and error, is exactly reproduced in all of them alike, without feeling convinced that *there must have been some one document with these peculiarities which was made the archetype or standard of the Massoretic text.* Where did this mysterious document come from? Was it a manuscript made by the men of the Great Synagogue as the result of revision? Was it one of the "Temple copies" referred to in p. 81? Was it a "Codex of Ezra," such as tradition tells of, or a standard selected in conclave by the Scribes? Or had it another and more tragic story— some dread crisis in the history of the nation—in the struggle with Antiochus—in the massacre at Bethur? Is there a lost picture somewhere in the ancient story —the hunted patriots hiding in the mountains; the soiled and torn fragments of the Hebrew manuscripts gathered together from their places of concealment, of some of the books only two or three, of some perhaps but a single copy, stained with blood, shrivelled by fire, all that remains to them of their sacred records?

What wonder if it were so in those awful days when the Bible so nearly perished altogether! What wonder if from these few manuscripts came the "Standard Bible," the ancestor of this mysteriously uniform text?

These are all but guesses, reader. We can only guess. The dim past holds its secret still as to the origin of this "Standard Bible."

CHAPTER IX.

AFTER the dispersion of the Jewish academies many Hebrew scholars fled to Europe, especially to Spain, where the critical study of the Bible and tradition was still carried on   The result of their work, however, is not to us of much importance, since the text was long before this time completely fixed.   Their writings are chiefly of value on account of the manuscripts which they had before them, many of which have since been lost to the world.

.   .   .   .   .   .

Amongst the famous names of this period often met with in Commentaries on the Bible are those of Aben-Ezra, Rashi, David Kimchi, and the great Maimonides, the Jewish Luther, of whom it is written, " From Moses of Sinai to Moses Maimonides, no man like him lived."

.   .   .   .   .   .

The first printed portion of the Hebrew Scripture was the Book of Psalms, published A.D. 1477.

.   .   .   .   .   .

The most important of all the earlier Hebrew Bibles
was issued in the sixteenth century by Daniel Bomberg of Venice, whose editor-in-chief was a very
famous scholar, the Rabbi Jacob - ben - Chajim, an
African Jew. It is most refreshing to watch this old
Hebrew's enthusiasm over his work, and to note, even in
so dry a document as an "Introduction to the Rabbinical Bible," the little touches revealing his character
and his moral fitness for so important a task. He is
greatly delighted with his employer's zeal. "Seignior
Daniel Bomberg," he writes, "did all in his power to
send into all countries in order to search what may be
found of the Massorah. He was not backward, nor
did he draw back his right hand from producing gold
out of his purse to defray the expenses of books and
messengers. . . . Like a bear bereft of her young
ones, he hastened to this work, for he loved the
daughter of Jacob."

A beautiful trait in his character is his simple
modesty so indicative of a superior mind. When
Bomberg proposed to him this great work, "I told
him," he says, "that I did not know as much as
he thought, in accordance with what we read at the
end of chap. ii. of the Jerusalem Maccoth, 'A man
who knows only one book when he is in a place
where he is respected for knowing two is in duty
bound to say, 'I know only one book.'"

It is rather amusing to compare the modesty of
ben Chajim with that of another great contemporary
worker at the Massorah notes, Elias Levita, whose

name has already occurred in the preceding pages.
"I have seen," he says, "that it is not good for this
my book to be alone. I will therefore make it an
helpmeet for it." And so he writes a poetical introduction in which he tells how people could not understand the Massoretic notes :—

"Till the day it was said to me by my estimable friends,
'What doest thou here, Elias? Throw light upon the Massorah.
For the glory of God and Holy Writ explain to us the Massorah.'
When the Prince heard me, then he kissed me with the kisses
of his mouth,
Saying, 'Art thou that my lord Elias whose books are over
all countries?'"

.   .   .   .   .   .

After Bomberg's Bible comes a long series of editions reaching down to the present century. Much
time and money and labour were expended in collecting and comparing Hebrew manuscripts for the preparation of the Bibles, but the result was very dis-
appointing. No discoveries of any importance were
made; nothing earlier than the Massoretic manuscripts
could anywhere be found, and these were almost word
for word the same.

.   .   .   .   .   .

Would you care to be shown, reader, an ancient
picture of the making of the "Standard Hebrew
Bible," [1] whose origin is enveloped in mystery, whose
manuscripts have been copied with such scrupulous
care that even its little flaws have come down to

[1] See Chap. VIII. p. 106.

us untouched? The picture rises irresistibly before
me from a page of my English Bible.

There is the old copyist seated at his desk patiently
transcribing letter by letter the wearisome list of names
in I Chron. viii., ix.—name after name—name after
name—in monotonous succession. At last he stops
and lays down his pen. He has just written the
words, "THESE DWELT AT JERUSALEM." · This will
do nicely for a catch-word to find his place again
when he returns, and so repeating the words to himself the old man retires to rest.

I see him next day resuming his task. He arranges
his parchments, he looks at the.catch-word, the last he
has written, and raising his eyes to the manuscript
before him, they light on the words, *but at the top of
the preceding page,* "THESE DWELT AT JERUSALEM,"
and calmly he goes on from that, in blissful uncon-
sciousness that he is writing over again his yesterday's
work.

You can find that little picture for yourself, my
reader, if you open your English Bible at I Chron.
ix. 34. This is the verse where the old scribe stopped
at "THESE DWELT AT JERUSALEM ; " and if you look up
to the 28th verse of the preceding chapter, you will
find the same words in the line that caught his eye
when he returned, and you will see he has written
over again after ix. 34 a good deal of the passage
that follows viii. 28.

.   .   .   .   .   .

Compared with the vast amount of labour expended

on the textual criticism of the New Testament, very little indeed has been done for the Old. Unfortunately, when the question of the perfect accuracy of the Old Testament text was first started in the Reformation days, it became at once, like that of the vowel-points, a party contest instead of an unbiassed search for the truth. The good fathers of the Council of Trent, innocent of any knowledge of Hebrew themselves, and desirous to laud up the authority of the (Latin) Vulgate, the Authorised Version of the Western Church of that day, threw doubts upon the correct transmission of the Hebrew manuscripts in the hands of the " unbelieving Jews." This, of course, was quite enough to rouse the Protestants to the defence of it, so that the accuracy of the Hebrew Old Testament soon became with them almost an article of faith, and, like many of the party shibboleths of to-day, was most violently insisted on by those who were least capable of forming a judgment about it. His " views were unsound," he was " tending to Popery," who openly expressed his doubts upon the question, and so the *odium theologicum*, as so often before and since, muzzled the honest seeking for the truth, and the unbiassed scholarly study of the subject was thrown back for centuries.

. . . . . .

Though much has been already done we have still great need of a good critical edition of the Old Testament, embodying the chief results of modern scholarship. There is, of course, in the absence of all manuscripts of earlier than Massoretic times, a great drawback to the critical study of the Old Testament, as compared with the New. But much more might be done with the material at hand, especially with the ancient versions, which, if thoroughly investigated, are capable of throwing much light upon the Hebrew text. There is reason to hope that our own generation will not be entirely unfruitful in this direction. We are promised very soon Dr. Ginsburg's critical edition of the Massoretic text; the Bishop of Salisbury is busy with the Vulgate of the New Testament, which we trust will soon be followed by that of the Old. Swete's scholarly edition of the Septuagint is in course of completion, and students are already busying themselves with the great treasury of Syriac manuscripts stored up in the library of the British Museum and elsewhere. But many years must elapse before any important results are attained in the investigation of the Hebrew Scriptures. The recent revision of the Old Testament was undertaken at least half-a-century too soon.

.   .   .   .   .   .

As to the right attitude to adopt with regard to the present Hebrew text, we may say that the best scholars receive it without hesitation as substantially accurate, at the same time leaving themselves open to accept any really well-authenticated corrections by means of the ancient versions.

.   .   .   .   .   .

In speaking thus plainly about the probability of errors in the Scriptures, there is great danger that an exaggerated impression should be caused as to the extent of these errors. The reader should be reminded that the great majority are of the most trivial kind, misspelling or transposing of words, omitting or inserting of insignificant particles, and such like. The New Testament variations are enormously more in number than those which probably will ever be discovered in the Old, and yet two of our greatest textual critics have asserted in a recent famous book[1] that the New Testament variations of any importance, if all put together, would not exceed the *one-thousandth* part of the whole text.

. . . . . .

Some readers will perhaps be disturbed at finding that the Old Testament has not been transmitted to us absolutely word for word correct. Well, such is the case anyhow; and whether we like it or no, there is no use in quarrelling with facts. We know with certainty that we have the *substance* of God's revelation exactly as the original writers had it; that we cannot say the same of every letter and syllable is surely not of so very much account. And perhaps it may not be altogether an unmixed evil either. It may help men to broader and truer notions of what inspiration really means. It may teach that not the ignorant worship of the letter, but the honest learning and obeying of the spirit of His revelation is what God values, since He has left the words of the Bible in some degree to run the same risks as the words of other books, while taking care that its substance should come down to us

[1] Westcott and Hort's Introduction to the Greek New Testament.

II

as originally given. It is surely instructive to see our Lord and His apostles content to use a Bible (the Septuagint) which, while giving faithfully the substance of God's Word, was often very inaccurate in minor details. We have a much more accurate Bible than they. But whatever our feeling about the matter, we should remember that we have it *as God has thought fit to let us have it.* Had it been necessary to His purposes that the text should have been miraculously preserved from the slightest flaw, we need have no doubt but that this would have been accomplished.

Book II.

THE OTHER OLD DOCUMENTS,

AND THEIR USE IN

BIBLICAL CRITICISM.

INTRODUCTION.

HAVING now learned something of the history and present condition of the "Old Hebrew Documents," we have next to examine some of the "Other Old Documents," *i.e.*, the various ancient Bibles which are used by critics in the investigation of the Hebrew text.

The reader will easily understand from the previous history the importance of these Bibles. All the old Hebrew manuscripts before A.D. 900 have vanished from the earth; unless in the very improbable event of some future romantic discovery in tombs or buried cities, we shall never be able to examine one of them. But these ancient Bibles were translated from those old vanished manuscripts ages and ages ago. Therefore the interrogating of them is like going back a thousand years behind our existing manuscripts and asking the men of our Lord's day, and even of long before, "How did that vanished old Hebrew Bible of yours read this or that disputed passage?"

Unfortunately, the value of *their* evidence also is lessened, as might be expected, by the same slips and errors of copyists whose existence in the Hebrew Bible has sent us to seek their aid. In the following pages we shall deal with the more important of these ancient Bibles.

I.

The Holy Manuscript of Nablous.

It had often been noticed with some curiosity, especially at the Reformation times, in the disputes about the Hebrew Bible, that in the works of certain old fathers, Origen, and St. Jerome, and Eusebius the historian, and others, there were references to "*the ancient Hebrew according to the Samaritans,*" as distinguished from the " Hebrew according to the Jews," and notes made of certain discrepancies existing between them. What could these references mean? No one in Europe knew anything about a " Samaritan Hebrew." Was it merely an error of these ancient fathers, or did there somewhere exist a Hebrew Bible differing from that which had come down to us through the Jews?

As time went on and nothing was discovered about it, it gradually began to be forgotten or relegated to the region of ancient fiction; until one day, early in the seventeenth century, when Biblical students were startled by the announcement that a copy of this mysterious document had arrived in Europe, having been discovered by a traveller among the Samaritans of Damascus.

It was a very venerable-looking manuscript, written in the unfamiliar ancient Hebrew letters, and for that reason at first very difficult to read.

Soon afterwards another copy was found in Egypt, but was captured by pirates, with the ship that was bringing it to Europe. Before 1630 Archbishop Ussher had obtained six others, and now there are altogether about sixteen Samaritan manuscripts in the European libraries.

The most famous copy in existence is the Synagogue Roll at Nablous, where the Samaritans, now but a few hundred in number, still cling to the ancient seat of their race.[1] It is guarded with the most sacred care, and never exhibited even to their own people, except on the Great Day of Atonement. A few Europeans have, however, managed to get a sight of it, and from their accounts we learn that the writing, which seems very old, is on the hair-side of skins twenty-five inches by fifteen—according to the Samaritan account, the skins of rams offered in sacrifice. The manuscript is worn very thin, even into holes in many places, and it is a good deal messed, as if with ink spilled over it, so that a large part is almost illegible. It is kept in a cylindrical silver case, ornamented with engravings of the Tabernacle and its furniture, and the whole is

---

[1] Nablous, a corruption of Neapolis, is almost on the site of ancient Shechem.

wrapped in a gorgeously embroidered cover of red satin and gold. The Samaritans assert that it is nearly as old as the days of Moses. They say—and one Russian traveller asserts that they are right—that an inscription runs through the middle of the text of the Ten Commandments :—

> I ABISHUA, SON OF PHINEHAS, SON OF ELEAZAR SON
> OF AARON THE PRIEST—UPON THEM BE THE GRACE
> OF JEHOVAH ! To HIS HONOUR HAVE I WRITTEN
> THIS HOLY LAW AT THE ENTRANCE OF THE TABERNACLE
> OF TESTIMONY ON MOUNT GERIZIM, BETH EL, IN
> THE THIRTEENTH YEAR OF THE TAKING POSSESSION OF
> THE LAND OF CANAAN. PRAISE JEHOVAH !

The inscription, however, has been looked for since, but in vain. Without entering too minutely into the question, all that we need say here is, that if it is or ever was in the manuscript, it does not deserve the slightest credit. Nobody who knows anything of the subject would believe that this manuscript has been in existence three thousand years.

II.

"Decline and Fall" of the Samaritan Bible.

Of course, these very ancient-looking manuscripts, when they first appeared, created a considerable sensation. Men talked of their use among scholars of Origen's days, of their strange ancient writing dating back beyond Ezra the Scribe, and with the usual tendency of human nature under such circumstances, many jumped at once to the conclusion that they had

THE SAMARITAN ROLL AT NABLOUS.

(*By kind permission of the Palestine Exploration Fund.*)

[To face page 120.]

got back to a document of vast antiquity, and that the received Hebrew text was of little account beside it.

Of course, too, like the other Biblical disputes referred to already, indeed like most theological disputes of those days when party spirit ran so high, the question as to their value soon became a contest for victory of party. The Romanist theologians made it almost a point of honour to uphold the Samaritan Scriptures. In the first place, they had always a strong prejudice against the Hebrew Bible. Not one of the good fathers of the Council of Trent knew a word of Hebrew, and they did not like its being set up as an authority against their Latin Vulgate Bible, the "Authorised Version" of the Western Church. Besides, it scored a point for them against Protestants if they could show that there was any uncertainty as to the text of the received Bible on which Protestants professed to take their stand—it proved the need of an infallible guide, which of course existed only in the Church of Rome. The Protestants were not slow in following the controversial lead thus set them, and so, instead of critically examining the Samaritan credentials with patient scholarly care, both parties contented themselves with fighting for victory and vigorously abusing their opponents.

This is no place for a critical treatment of the question. Suffice it to say, that when the din of controversy had ceased sufficiently for calmer arguments to be heard, the opinion of scholars gradually grew against the authority of the Samaritan text, though still they were willing to allow a good deal of weight to its variations from the Hebrew. At length, early in the present century, even the remnant of authority remaining to it was quite swept away. A great Hebrew scholar, Gesenius, having analysed and classified its deviations from the Jewish manuscripts, showed in a masterly essay that they were nearly all owing to—(1) grammatical blunders of the Samaritan Scribes; or (2) to a disposition to smooth and explain readings that seemed to them difficult and obscure; or (3) to a wilful corruption of the text for controversial purposes, as, for example, where they substitute for the name of Ebal that of Mount Gerizim, on which their schismatical Temple stood, to show that this was the spot indicated by God as the future national place of worship. We may add that, so unanswerable are the arguments in this treatise, no one now would think of setting up the Samaritan Pentateuch as an authority in Biblical criticism.

III.

Its Use in Criticism.

Yet is it of some value in criticising our Hebrew Bible. With all its faults, it has at least this in its favour as an independent witness, that its text has been kept for nearly twenty-five centuries free from any contact with the received Jewish text. Therefore, its substantial agreement through its whole extent with the Massoretic manuscripts is a clear proof of their general accuracy. On the other hand, if, in some minor detail, the Syriac and Vulgate and other important ancient Bibles to be described hereafter agree with each other against a reading in the Jewish Bible, it is evident that their case would be considerably strengthened if we found the Samaritan on their side, as in the examples already given (p. 52), "Cain said unto Abel, Let us go into the field" (Gen. iv. 8), or Joseph "made bondmen" of the people of Egypt (Gen. xlvii. 21). Here the Septuagint and Syriac and Vulgate agree against the Hebrew; and when we turn to the Samaritan we find it agreeing with them, thus making a strong case against the accuracy of the received text in these places.

There is a well-known variation in Exod. xii. 40, where the Hebrew text tells that "the sojourning of the children of Israel who dwelt in Egypt was 430 years." If the writer meant that their sojourning *in Egypt* was 430 years, it seems difficult to reconcile it with the chronology or with St. Paul's statement in Gal. iii. 17, where 430 years is given as the whole interval between Abraham and the Lawgiving on Mount Sinai. The Samaritan has, "The sojourning of the children of Israel *and of their fathers in the land of Canaan and* in the land of Egypt was 430 years."[1] It may be that the Samaritan is right, but from what we know of its general character, it is not at all improbable that this is a correction to remove what seemed to its editors a chronological difficulty.

[1] And the Septuagint has substantially the same. Yet there are forcible arguments on the other side, and Egyptologists say that the Egyptian chronology seems to confirm our received reading.

The reading seems a very tempting one, but most Biblical critics refuse to accept it. It is a good illustration of the rule in p. 25, that in many cases " the more difficult of two readings must be preferred to the easier."

V.

A Roundabout Story-teller.

The reader must not think that because the Samaritan is of little authority in its *variations* from the Jewish Pentateuch, it is therefore a very corrupt and valueless book. Nothing of the kind. If we had not the Jewish text we should not be at all badly off with the " Five Books of Moses, according to the Samaritans." The variations for the most part consist of unimportant mistakes of grammar, and of expansions and paraphrases which very little affect the meaning. One curious peculiarity is, that when there is recorded some long command of God to Moses, whereas the Jewish text would briefly tell that Moses did as he was commanded, the Samaritan must needs go over the whole command, word for word, in recording that Moses had done it.

It may interest the reader to have a specimen from this famous old document. I select the following passage because it illustrates, amongst other things, the peculiarity I have just referred to. It will be noticed that it agrees substantially with the Hebrew, its only variation being that it repeats almost word for word the second paragraph in recording how literally Moses and Aaron did as they were commanded :—

HEBREW.

AND THE LORD SAID UNTO MOSES, PHARAOH'S HEART IS HARDENED, HE REFUSETH TO LET THE PEOPLE GO. GET THEE UNTO PHARAOH IN THE MORNING ; LO, HE GOETH UNTO THE WATER ; AND THOU SHALT STAND BY THE RIVER'S BRINK AGAINST HE COME ; AND THE ROD WHICH WAS TURNED TO A SERPENT SHALT THOU TAKE IN THINE HAND.

AND THOU SHALT SAY UNTO HIM, THE LORD GOD OF THE HEBREWS HATH SENT ME UNTO THEE, SAYING, LET MY PEOPLE GO, THAT THEY MAY SERVE ME IN THE WILDERNESS : AND, BEHOLD, HITHERTO THOU WOULDEST NOT HEAR. THUS SAITH THE LORD, IN THIS THOU SHALT KNOW THAT I AM THE LORD : BEHOLD, I WILL SMITE WITH THE ROD THAT IS IN MINE HAND UPON THE WATERS WHICH ARE IN THE RIVER, AND THEY SHALL BE TURNED INTO BLOOD. AND THE FISH THAT IS IN THE RIVER SHALL DIE, AND THE RIVER SHALL STINK ; AND THE EGYPTIANS SHALL LOATHE TO DRINK OF THE WATER OF THE RIVER.

AND THE LORD SPAKE UNTO MOSES, SAY UNTO AARON, TAKE THY ROD, AND STRETCH OUT THINE HAND UPON THE WATERS OF EGYPT, &c.—EXOD. vii. 14-19.

SAMARITAN.

AND THE LORD SAID UNTO MOSES, PHARAOH'S HEART IS HARDENED, HE REFUSETH TO LET THE PEOPLE GO. GET THEE UNTO PHARAOH IN THE MORNING ; LO, HE GOETH UNTO THE WATER ; AND THOU SHALT STAND BY THE RIVER'S BRINK AGAINST HE COME ; AND THE ROD WHICH WAS TURNED TO A SERPENT SHALT THOU TAKE IN THINE HAND.

AND THOU SHALT SAY UNTO HIM, THE LORD GOD OF THE HEBREWS HATH SENT ME UNTO THEE, SAYING, LET MY PEOPLE GO, THAT THEY MAY SERVE ME IN THE WILDERNESS : AND, BEHOLD, HITHERTO THOU WOULDEST NOT HEAR. THUS SAITH THE LORD, IN THIS THOU SHALT KNOW THAT I AM THE LORD : BEHOLD, I WILL SMITE WITH THE ROD THAT IS IN MINE HAND UPON THE WATERS WHICH ARE IN THE RIVER, AND THEY SHALL BE TURNED INTO BLOOD. AND THE FISH THAT IS IN THE RIVER SHALL DIE, AND THE RIVER SHALL STINK ; AND THE EGYPTIANS SHALL LOATHE TO DRINK OF THE WATER OF THE RIVER.

AND MOSES AND AARON WENT TO PHARAOH, AND SAID UNTO HIM, THE LORD GOD OF THE HEBREWS HATH SENT US TO THEE, SAYING, LET MY PEOPLE GO, THAT THEY MAY SERVE ME IN THE WILDERNESS : AND, BEHOLD, HITHERTO THOU WOULDEST NOT HEAR. THUS SAITH THE LORD, IN THIS THOU SHALT KNOW THAT I AM THE LORD : BEHOLD, I WILL SMITE WITH THE ROD THAT IS IN MINE HAND UPON THE WATERS WHICH ARE IN THE RIVER, AND THEY SHALL BE TURNED INTO BLOOD. AND THE FISH THAT IS IN THE RIVER SHALL DIE, AND THE RIVER SHALL STINK ; AND THE EGYPTIANS SHALL LOATHE TO DRINK OF THE WATER OF THE RIVER.

AND THE LORD SPAKE UNTO MOSES, SAY UNTO AARON, TAKE THY ROD, AND STRETCH OUT THINE HAND UPON THE WATERS OF EGYPT, &c.

DOCUMENTS No. II.

THE TALMUD AND THE TARGUMS.

HERE we bring together a group of documents not of sufficient importance to be separately treated.

THE TALMUD.

I.

What is the Talmud?

We have already seen (Bk. i. p. 79) that from time immemorial there existed amongst the Jews certain oral traditions about the Scriptures and their interpretation; that these, handed down through many generations, were at length, in the early centuries of Christianity, collected and systematised in the colleges of the Scribes into a book called the MISHNA; that in course of time a "Gemara," or Commentary, was written on this book; and that the Mishna, together with its Gemara, make up what is called the TALMUD. We may add here that the writing down of the Mishna occurred about the second century A.D., and that of the Gemara about the fourth or fifth.[1] It is evident that

---

[1] The Gemara, or Commentary of Jerusalem, dates about 370 A.D., and that of the Babylon schools about 500 A.D. According as the Jerusalem or Babylon Gemara was attached to the Mishna, so the whole was called the Jerusalem or Babylon Talmud.

such a book as this must necessarily contain a great many quotations from Scripture, often involving minute reference to the exact words of the text, and therefore that it ought to be one of the most valuable aids in testing the accuracy of the existing manuscripts.

Unfortunately, however, owing to the extreme reverence of the Jews for the Massoretic text, the successive editors of the Talmud seem to have altered its quotations to correspond with the Hebrew manuscripts before them, so that the most careful examination of the existing Talmud copies have led to no discoveries of much importance. True, there are recorded about a thousand variations from the existing Bible, but very few of them are of any consequence. Therefore, it will be seen that the Talmud cannot be expected to count for much in the aids to Bible criticism.

This is all that is absolutely necessary to be said about the Talmud for the purpose of this present work, but it is impossible here to lay down the pen. Indeed, it would be scarcely justifiable to dismiss in a few pages a book that stands out so prominently in the history of Judaism—nay, I should rather say in the history of the world. Who has not heard of the " Talmud," and formed some puzzled notion as to what the word means ? Continually it meets us in all classes of reading. In science, in literature, in theology, in law, in ethics, in metaphysics, in ancient fairy-lore, the old-world name arises to us again and again, making us wonder what the curious treatise can be that touches in so many points such varied subjects.

It is, therefore, worth while writing a little further about the Talmud. One is sorely tempted to wander off into whole chapters on its fascinating lore. So if we promise to reasonably restrain our vagrant impulses, the reader, we hope, will pardon a few pages more, even if not absolutely necessary to our "Lesson in Biblical Criticism."

II.

Conflicting Opinions.

Very varied are the opinions about the Talmud. Christian writers, with whom it has been too much the custom to read non-Christian books with the object of refuting them, have given us many treatises branding it as the very curse of Judaism and of religion. They have dwelt upon our Lord's condemning its traditions. They have collected from it samples torn out of their context, silly and grotesque stories, conflicting statements, and specimens of the ignorant and narrow prejudices of the nation. They have declaimed against its legendary colouring of Bible narratives—its profane and degrading representations of God, the Almighty and His angels taking part in foolish discussions of the Rabbis. They have held up their hands in horror at indelicate allusions such as they could not dare to transfer to their pages.

And all these charges can be fully proved against the Talmud. In its vast and tangled mass of ancient lore many such evil things as these can be found. Indeed, at times, the reader, wandering through the pages of nonsense that these wise sages wrote, will feel almost a sympathy with the belief of Carlyle, that " nine out of every ten men are fools, and he would not like to say too much about the tenth." But to dwell only on these faults would be to give a very false impression of this wonderful old book, some parts of which have come down to us from almost the dawn of antiquity.

It should be remembered that our Lord Himself, like all other Jewish boys, was probably, in His childhood, taught from the Talmud ; that many of our household words in theology have come to us, through Him, from the Talmud teaching. Redemption, Baptism, Grace, Salvation, Faith, Son of Man, &c., are words of old Judaism, to which He only gave a higher meaning. His rebukes, too, were directed only against its faults, not against its whole substance. The Talmud itself speaks almost as strongly as He against the " plague of Pharisaism ;" the " dyed ones who do evil deeds like Zimri, and require a goodly reward like Phinehas ;" " who preach beautifully, but do not act beautifully." The Talmud points to the Scriptures as the source of all teaching. " Turn them, and turn them again," it says, for " everything is in them." Six hundred and thirteen injunctions, says the Talmud, was Moses directed to give to the people. David reduced them to eleven in the 15th Psalm : " He that walketh uprightly," &c. The prophet Micah reduced them to three : " What doth the Lord require of thee, but to do justly, and to love mercy, and to walk humbly with thy God ? " (vi. 8). Amos

I

reduced them to one: " Seek ye Me and ye shall live " (v. 4).

Therefore it is that the Jews indignantly challenge the Christian accounts of this their greatest literary treasure next to the Bible. They point to its enforcing and explaining the Scriptures; to its mighty influence in preserving their nationality; to its wholesome directions about purity and cleanliness; to its result in many a social excellence in the character of their nation. " Nothing," say they, " can absolve the Jews from the debt of gratitude which they owe to the Talmud, the book which in so great measure has helped to make them what they are."

III.

"Law and Legend."

To understand these conflicting testimonies, it is important to keep in mind, what has been too often overlooked, that the Talmud consists of two elements, LAW and LEGEND, Halachah and Hagadah, as they are called by the Jews.

The former is an attempt to bring the Mosaic legislation into practical operation—that is, to bring under its great principles the little ordinary cases of everyday life. This is often done in a foolish and quibbling manner; it often goes into indelicate details in order to be thoroughly practical; it often, too, must be charged with making void the Word of God by its refinements of fanciful exposition. Yet no man who studies the history of the Jews can doubt, on the whole, its important influence for good upon the nation.

The other or Legendary element consists of a series of anecdotes and sayings of the scribes, a kind of ornamental addition illustrating and enforcing the principles of the Law, or affectionately commemorating the great sages of the past. To us stolid children of the West it must seem often but a wild play of fancy and fable and humour not very much in keeping with the solemnity of its purpose; but to the Jews, who know it best, it is a store of wise and tender and touching sayings; its allegories and parables and fairy-lore, even where they seem to us the most foolish, being credited with a lofty and beautiful secret meaning. And even our duller vision can perceive that many of its stories and moral precepts are exquisitely beautiful, and cannot fail to be helpful to the Jewish children, who are taught them from their earliest days.

IV.

Talmud Sayings.

In the following section I give some specimens from the Talmud. But it is necessary to guard the reader against forming from them too favourable an impression. He must remember that they are specimens of the Talmud *at its best*, and that often a considerable mass of rubbish has to be waded through to find them :—

Jerusalem was destroyed because the instruction of the young was neglected.

· · · · · · ·

The world is saved by the breath of the school-children. Even for the rebuilding of the Temple, schools must not be interrupted.

· · · · · · ·

A sage, walking in the crowded market-place, suddenly encountered the prophet Elijah. "Who out of that crowd shall be saved?" he asked; and Elijah pointed to a poor turnkey, "Because he was merciful to his prisoners;" and next to two common workmen pleasantly talking as they passed. The sage rushed up to them and asked, "I pray you, what are your saving works?" But the puzzled workmen replied, "We are poor men who live by our trade. We know not of any good works in us. We try to be cheerful and good-natured. We talk to the sad, and cheer them to forget their grief. If we know of two who have quarrelled, we talk to them, and persuade them to be friends. This is our whole life."

· · · · · · ·

Life is a passing shadow, says the Scripture. Is it the shadow of a tower or of a tree? A shadow that prevails for a while? Nay, it is the shadow of a bird in his flight; away flies the bird, and there is neither bird nor shadow.

· · · · · · ·

He who has more learning than good works is like a tree with many branches but few roots, which the first wind throws on its face; while he whose good works are greater than his knowledge is like a tree with many roots and few branches, which all the winds of heaven cannot uproot.

· · · · · · ·

Teach thy tongue to say, "I do not know."

· · · · · · ·

Prayer is Israel's only weapon, a weapon inherited from its fathers and tried in a thousand battles.

· · · · · · ·

Moses made a serpent of brass and put it on a pole; and it came to pass, if a serpent had bitten any man, when he beheld that serpent of brass he lived. Dost think that a serpent killeth or giveth life? But as long as Israel are looking up to their Father in Heaven they will not die.

.   .   .   .

We read that while, in the contest with Amalek, Moses lifted up his arms Israel prevailed. Did Moses' hands make war or break war? But this is to tell you that as long as Israel are looking upwards and humbling their hearts before the Father in Heaven they will prevail; if not, they fall.

.   .   .   .

"If your God hates idolatry," asked a heathen, "why does He not destroy it?" And they answered him, "Behold, men worship the sun, the moon, the stars. Would you have Him destroy this beautiful world for the sake of the foolish?"

.   .   .   .

If there is anything bad to say of you, say it yourself.

.   .   .   .

Commit a sin twice and you will think it quite allowable.

.   .   .   .

Think of three things, whence thou comest, whither thou goest, and to whom thou shalt have to give account, even the All Holy, praised be He! Four shall not enter into Paradise : the scoffer, the liar, the hypocrite, and the slanderer. To slander is to murder.

.   .   .   .

Love your wife like yourself; honour her more than yourself. Whoever lives unmarried lives without joy, without comfort, without blessing. Descend a step in choosing a wife. If she be small, bend down to her and whisper in her ear. He who forsakes the love of his youth, God's altar weeps for him. He who sees his wife die before him has, as it were, been present at the destruction of the sanctuary itself—the world grows dark around him.

.   .   .   .

It is woman alone through which God's blessings are vouchsafed to a house. She teaches the children, speeds the husband to the place of worship, and welcomes him when he returns ; she keeps the house godly and pure, and God's blessing rests on all these things.

He who marries for money, his children shall be a curse to him.

The house that does not open to the poor shall open to the physician.

The day is short and the work is heavy, but the labourers are idle, though the reward be great. It is not incumbent on thee to complete the work, but thou must not therefore cease from it. If thou hast worked much great shall be thy reward, for the Master who employed thee is faithful in His payment. But know that the true reward is not of this world.

A man stands at the door of his patron's house. He dare not ask for the patron himself, but for his favourite slave or his son, who then goes in and tells the master inside, "This man, N. N., is standing at the gate ; shall he come in or not?" Not so the Holy ; praised be He ! If misfortune come upon a man, let him not cry to Michael or to Gabriel, but unto Me let him cry, and I will answer him right speedily, as it is written, Every one who calls on the name of the Lord shall be saved.

V.

Bible Commentary.

Here are a few specimens of its Bible commentary :—

Cain was ploughing his fields. Abel, leading his flocks to pasture, crossed the ground which his brother was tilling.

In a wrathful spirit, Cain approached Abel, saying, "Wherefore comest thou with thy flocks to dwell in and to feed upon the land which belongs to me ?"

And Abel answered, "Wherefore eatest thou of the flesh of my sheep? Wherefore clothe thyself in garments fashioned from their wool ? Pay me for the flesh which thou hast eaten, for the garments in which thou art clothed, for they are mine, even as this ground is thine."

Then said Cain to his brother, "Behold, thou art in my power. If I should see fit to slay thee now, to-day, who would avenge thy death?"

"God, who has placed us upon this earth," replied Abel. "He is the judge who rewardeth the pious man according to his deeds, and the wicked according to his wickedness. Thou canst not slay me and hide from Him the action. He will surely punish thee; ay, even for the evil words which thou hast spoken to me but now."

This answer increased Cain's wrathful feelings, and raising the implement of his labour which he was holding in his hand, he struck his brother suddenly therewith and killed him. And it came to pass after this rash action that Cain grieved and wept bitterly. Then arising, he dug a hole in the ground and buried therein his brother's body from the light of day.

And after this, the Lord appeared to Cain and said to him—

"**Where is Abel thy brother,** who was with thee?"

And Cain replied unto the Lord—

"**I know not. Am I my brother's keeper?**"

Then said the Lord—

"**What hast thou done? Thy brother's blood cries to Me from the ground.**"

.   .   .   .

Abram, when quite a child, beholding the brilliant splendour of the noonday sun and the reflected glory which it cast upon all objects around, he said, "Surely this brilliant light must be a god; to him will I render worship." And he worshipped the sun and prayed to it. But as the day lengthened the sun's brightness faded, the radiance which it cast upon the earth was lost in the lowering clouds of night, and as the twilight deepened the youth ceased his supplication, saying, "No, this cannot be a god. Where then can I find the Creator, He who made the heavens and the earth?" He looked towards the west, the south, the north, and to the east. The sun disappeared from his view; nature became enveloped in the pall of a past day. Then the moon arose, and when Abram saw it shining in the heavens surrounded by its myriads of stars, he said, "Perhaps these are the gods who have created all things," and he uttered prayers to them. But when the morning dawned and the stars paled, and the moon faded into silvery whiteness and was lost in the returning glory of the sun, Abram knew God, and said, "There is a higher power, a Supreme Being, and these luminaries are but His servants, the work of His hands." From that day, even until the day of his death, Abram knew the Lord, and walked in all His ways. And Abram sought his father when he was surrounded by his officers, and he spoke to him, saying—

"Father tell me, I pray, where I may find the God who created the heavens and the earth, thee, and me, and all the people in the world."

And Terah answered, "My son, the creator of all things is here with us in the house."

Then said Abram, "Show him to me, my father."

And Terah led Abram into an inner apartment, and pointing to the twelve large idols and the many smaller ones around, he said, "These are the gods who created the heavens and the earth, thee, me, and all the people of the world."

Abram then sought his mother, saying, "My mother, behold, my father has shown to me the gods who created the earth and all that it contains ; therefore prepare for me, I pray thee, a kid for a sacrifice, that the gods of my father may partake of the same and receive it favourably."

Abram's mother did as her son had requested her, and Abram placed the food which she prepared before the idols, but none stretched forth a hand to eat.

Then Abram jested, and said, "Perchance 'tis not exactly to their tastes, or mayhap the quantity appears stinted. I will prepare a larger offering, and strive to make it still more savoury."

Next day Abram requested his mother to prepare two kids, and with her greatest skill, and placing them before the idols, he watched, with the same result as on the previous day.

Then Abram exclaimed, "Woe to my father and to this evil generation ; woe to those who incline their hearts to vanity and worship senseless images without the power to smell or eat, to see or hear. Mouths they have, but sounds they cannot utter; eyes they have, but lack all power to see; they have ears that cannot hear, hands that cannot move, and feet that cannot walk. Senseless they are as the men who wrought them; senseless all who trust in them and bow before them." And seizing an iron implement, he destroyed and broke with it all the images save one, into the hands of which he placed the iron which he had used.

The noise of this proceeding reached the ears of Terah, who hurried to the apartment, where he found the broken idols and the food which Abram had placed before them. In wrath and indignation he cried out unto his son, saying, " What is this that thou hast done unto my gods?"

And Abram answered, " I brought them savoury food, and behold, they all grasped for it with eagerness at the same time, all save the largest one, who, annoyed and displeased with their greed, seized that iron which he holds and destroyed them."

" False are thy words," answered Terah in anger. " Had these images the breath of life, that they should move and act as thou hast said? Did I not fashion them with my own hands? How, then, could the larger destroy the smaller ones?"

" Then why serve senseless, powerless gods?" replied Abram; " gods who can neither help thee in thy need nor hear thy supplications?"

VI.

The Legend of Sandalphon.

Some of our readers will remember Longfellow's exquisite presentation of the ancient Talmud legend:—

SANDALPHON.

" Have you read in the Talmud of old,
In the legends the Rabbins have told,
Of the limitless realms of the air,—
Have you read it,—the marvellous story
Of Sandalphon, the Angel of Glory,
Sandalphon, the Angel of Prayer?

How erect at the outermost gates
Of the City Celestial he waits,
　With his feet on the ladder of light,
That, crowded with angels unnumbered,
By Jacob was seen as he slumbered
　Alone in the desert by night?

The Angels of Wind and of Fire
Chant only one hymn and expire
　With the song's irresistible stress ;
Expire in their rapture and wonder,
As harp-strings are broken asunder
　By music they throb to express !

But serene in the rapturous throng,
Unmoved by the rush of the song,
　With eyes unimpassioned and slow,
Among the dead angels, the deathless
Sandalphon stands listening breathless
　To sounds that ascend from below ;—

From the spirits on earth that adore ;
From the souls that entreat and implore
　In the fervour and passion of prayer ;
From the hearts that are broken with losses,
And weary from dragging the crosses
　Too heavy for mortals to bear.

And he gathers the prayers as he stands,
And they change into flowers in his hands,
　Into garlands of purple and red ;
And beneath the great arch of the portal,
Through the streets of the City Immortal,
　Is wafted the fragrance they shed.

It is but a legend, I know—
A fable, a phantom, a show
　Of the ancient Rabbinical lore ;

Yet the old mediæval tradition,
The beautiful, strange superstition,
But haunts me and holds me the more.

When I look from my window at night,
And the welkin above is all white,
  All throbbing and panting with stars,
Among them majestic is standing
Sandalphon the angel, expanding
  His pinions in nebulous bars.

And the legend, I feel, is a part
Of the hunger and thirst of the heart ;
  The frenzy and fire of the brain,
That grasps at the fruitage forbidden,
The golden pomegranates of Eden,
  To quiet its fever and pain." [1]

VII.

An Ancient "Rip Van Winkle."

The following illustration from the Babylonian
Talmud (*Taanith*, fol. 23 *a* and *b*) will show (1) how
Bible quotations occur which may be used for textual
criticism ; (2) the Rabbis' fanciful method of Bible

[1] Longfellow seems to have been a good deal attracted by the Talmud. There are few more beautiful things in his works than the Legend of the Rabbi ben Levi, who sprang over the walls of Heaven with the sword of the Angel of Death in his hand, and thus obtained for man the boon that the dread Angel must "walk on earth unseen for ever- more." The reader may remember in the "Golden Legend" the scene of the Rabbi and the school-children :—

> "Come hither, Judas Iscariot,
>   Say if thy lesson thou hast got
>   From the Rabbinical Book or not ?"

and how, after Judas has glibly answered in the great Talmud mys- teries, the old pedagogue proceeds to call up "little Jesus, the car penter's son."

interpretation; and, perhaps, (3) the origin of the
favourite fairy-tale, "The Sleeping Beauty," who slept
for seventy years, and of Washington Irving's famous
story of "Rip Van Winkle:"—

"Choni ha-Maagol was all his life unable to understand the
Biblical passage, '**When the Lord turned again the captivity
of Zion, we were like them that dream**' (Ps. cxxvi. 1). 'Can
seventy years be regarded as a dream? How is it possible,' he
asked, 'for a man to remain for seventy years asleep?' One
day, whilst on a journey, he saw a man planting a carob-tree, and
asked him how long a period he expected would elapse before
the tree became fruitful. 'Seventy years,' was the reply. 'Do
you then expect to live seventy years and to eat of the fruit?'
'When I entered the world,' was the answer, 'I found carob-
trees in abundance. Even as my fathers planted for me, in like
manner shall I also plant for those that are to come after me.'

"Choni sat down to his meal, and a deep sleep fell upon him,
and he slumbered. The rock closed up around him, and he was
hidden from the sight of men. And thus he lay for seventy
years. When he awoke and rose to his feet, lo! he beheld a
man eating of the fruit of the very carob-tree that he had seen
planted. Choni asked, 'Dost thou know who it was that planted
this tree?' 'My grandfather.' Then Choni knew that he had
slept on for seventy years. He went to his house and asked
where the son of Choni ha-Maagol was. 'His son,' they told
him, 'is dead. His grandson you can see if you will.' 'I am
Choni ha-Maagol!' he exclaimed; but no one believed him.

"He thence turned his steps to the House of Learning, and
he heard the Rabbis saying, 'We have resolved this difficulty
as we used to do when Choni ha-Maagol was alive;' for in
times past, when Choni went to the meeting, he was able to
expound every subject under discussion. 'I am Choni ha-
Maagol!' he cried for the second time. But again none would
believe him, neither did they treat him with honour. Broken-
hearted, he left the haunts of men, and prayed for death, and his
prayer was answered. 'This,' says Ravah, 'is the meaning of
the saying: To the friendless man Death cometh as a blessing.'"

VIII.

"The House that Jack Built."

It may seem strange to be looking in the holy books of the Jews for the origin of fairy-tales; but what would you say, my reader, if you found in them the source of "The House that Jack Built;" and, moreover, if you were told that this queer old nursery rhyme is but an adaptation of a solemn Passover hymn of ancient days, by means of which the Jewish children learned in parable the history of their nation? The poem is found in the Seder Hagadah (Passover Service-Book), fol. 23, 1831. It is translated from the Chaldee. I take the interpretation from the small edition published by Vallentyne, Bedford Square, London:—

I.

A kid, a kid, my father bought
For two pieces of money :
    A kid, a kid.

2.

Then came the cat, and ate the kid,
That my father bought
For two pieces of money :
    A kid, a kid.

3.

Then came the dog, and bit the cat,
That ate the kid,
That my father bought
For two pieces of money :
    A kid, a kid.

The *kid*, a clean animal, refers to Israel, "the one peculiar people upon earth," which God purchased (Exod. xv. 16) for Himself by means of the two precious tables of the Law.
The *cat* refers to Babylon. "Devoured the kid" is descriptive of the Babylonian captivity, which swallowed up Jewish nationality, A.M. 3338.

The *dog* means Persia, by whose power Babylon was overthrown.

4.

Then came the staff, and beat the dog,
That bit the cat,
That ate the kid,
That my father bought
For two pieces of money :
           A kid, a kid.

The *staff* is Greece, which put an end to the Persian domination.

5.

Then came the fire, and burned the staff,
That beat the dog,
That bit the cat,
That ate the kid,
That my father bought
For two pieces of money :
           A kid, a kid.

The *fire* refers to Rome.

6.

Then came the water, and quenched the
     fire,
That burned the staff,
That beat the dog,
That bit the cat,
That ate the kid,
That my father bought
For two pieces of money :
           A kid, a kid.

The *water* refers to the Turks, descendants of Ishmael, who wrested the Holy Land from the power of Rome.

7.

Then came the ox, and drank the water,
That quenched the fire,
That burned the staff,
That beat the dog,
That bit the cat,
That ate the kid,
That my father bought
For two pieces of money :
           A kid, a kid.

The *ox* means Edom (the European nations), who will in the latter days rescue the Holy Land from the possession of Ishmael. (See Abarbanel on Ezek. xxxix.)

8.

Then came the butcher, and slew the ox
That drank the water,
That quenched the fire,
That burned the staff,
That beat the dog,
That bit the cat,
That ate the kid,
That my father bought
For two pieces of money :
        A kid, a kid.

The *butcher* refers to the fearful war which will then succeed, when the confederated armies of Gog and Magog, Persia, Cush, and Pul will come up "like the tempest" to drive the sons of Edom from Palestine (Ezek. xxxviii., xxxix.).

9.

Then came the Angel of Death, and
    killed the butcher,
That slew the ox,
That drank the water,
That quenched the fire,
That burned the staff,
That beat the dog,
That bit the cat,
That ate the kid,
That my father bought
For two pieces of money :
        A kid, a kid.

The *Angel of Death* is a great pestilence, in which all the foes of Israel shall perish.

10.

Then came the Holy One, blessed be He !
And killed the Angel of Death,
That killed the butcher,
That slew the ox,
That drank the water,
That quenched the fire,
That burned the staff,
That beat the dog,
That bit the cat,
That ate the kid,
That my father bought
For two pieces of money :
        A kid, a kid.[1]

The last verse describes the establishment of God's kingdom on earth, when Israel shall be restored under Messiah, the son of David.

[1] It would seem as if from this ancestry came not only "The House

THE TARGUMS.

The Talmud has tempted us so far beyond our limits that very little space is left for dealing with the Targums, the Chaldee paraphrases of Scripture in use for the teaching of the people. The reader will remember the scene at p. 61, where Ezra read to the returned exiles from his manuscript of the Law, and the Scribes had to "give the sense and cause them to understand the reading." This is the first instance we have of a Targum or paraphrase. It afterwards became a regular custom in the synagogue, for the sake of the common people who had lost all knowledge of the holy tongue, that, when the words of the Law were read, an interpreter should translate into vernacular Aramaic, and that he should expand his translation into a free paraphrase of the meaning, that all the people might easily understand. This interpreter, or " meturgeman " (our English word " dragoman," which occurs so frequently in stories of modern Eastern travel), was bound by certain rules: he must wait till the reader had finished his verse or passage; neither reader nor meturgeman is to raise his voice one above the other; the meturgeman must not lean against a pillar or beam, but stand erect with fear and reverence; he must never use a written

that Jack Built," but also that other queer doggerel of the old woman and the kid, "Butcher, butcher, kill Ox, Ox will not drink Water, Water will not quench Fire, Fire will not burn Stick, Stick will not beat Kid, and I cannot get home till midnight."

"Targum," but must deliver his interpretation "ex-tempore," lest it might seem that he was reading out of the Law itself, and thus the Scriptures be held accountable for his teaching.

In course of time, however, the same causes which led to the writing of the Talmud led also to the per-mission that Targums might be written, and thus these paraphrases have come down to us to help in testing the accuracy of the text.

Their value for this purpose, however, is but small, not only on account of the loose and fanciful nature of their comments, but also because the oldest dates no farther back than the early Christian centuries, when the present Massoretic text was already pretty well established. Their freedom in dealing with the Scrip-tures makes it difficult to tell what were the exact words of the text which was being interpreted, but it is clear that the sacred manuscripts before them must have corresponded very closely with those in our hands to-day. The Targum of Onkelos on the Penta-teuch is the most valuable, owing to its keeping so literally to its text. There are, besides, the Targum of Jonathan, the Jerusalem Targum, and others, but it is not necessary to enter more fully into details. Perhaps the following little specimen may interest the reader, and give him a clearer idea of the use of the Targums for the purpose of textual criticism :—

BIBLE. GEN. III. 22.	TARGUM OF ONKELOS.	TARGUM OF JONATHAN.
AND THE LORD GOD SAID, BEHOLD, THE MAN IS BECOME AS ONE OF US, TO KNOW GOOD AND EVIL : AND NOW, LEST HE PUT FORTH HIS HAND, AND TAKE ALSO OF THE TREE OF LIFE, AND EAT, AND LIVE FOR EVER.	AND THE LORD GOD SAID, BEHOLD, ADAM IS THE ONLY ONE IN THE WORLD KNOWING GOOD AND EVIL : PERCHANCE NOW HE MIGHT STRETCH FORTH HIS HAND, AND TAKE ALSO FROM THE TREE OF LIFE, AND EAT, AND LIVE FOR EVERMORE.	AND THE LORD GOD SAID TO THE ANGELS THAT WERE MINISTERING BEFORE HIM, LO, THERE IS ADAM ALONE ON THE EARTH, AS I AM ALONE IN THE HIGHEST HEAVEN, AND THERE WILL SPRING FROM HIM THOSE WHO KNOW HOW TO DISTIN- GUISH BETWEEN GOOD AND EVIL. IF HE HAD KEPT THE COMMANDMENT THAT I COM- MANDED HE WOULD HAVE BEEN LIVING AND LASTING, LIKE THE TREE OF LIFE, FOR EVERMORE. NOW, SINCE HE HAS NOT KEPT WHAT I COM- MANDED, WE DECREE AGAINST HIM, AND EXPEL HIM FROM THE GARDEN OF EDEN, BE- FORE HE MAY STRETCH OUT HIS HAND AND TAKE FROM THE FRUITS OF THE TREE OF LIFE, FOR IF HE ATE THERE- FROM HE WOULD LIVE AND REMAIN FOR EVER.

DOCUMENT No. III.

I.

The Apostles' Bible.

We have now to tell of a very wonderful book, the most important as well as the most famous version of the Bible that the world has ever seen. It was the first translation of Holy Scripture in existence. It, and not the original Hebrew, was the Bible chiefly used by our Lord, the Bible used by the Apostles [1] and Evangelists, the Bible used by Jews and Gentiles alike in the early days of Christianity. It is the source of most of the ancient versions of the Old Testament. It supplies the chief theological terms of the New. It is to-day in the Eastern Church the standard, the sacred text, fully installed in the place of the original Hebrew.

This rival of the Hebrew Bible text was the celebrated Greek version of the Old Testament known as "THE SEPTUAGINT," or Bible of the Seventy, which in the two centuries before Christ was the recognised

---

[1] Out of thirty-seven quotations made by our Lord, thirty-three agree almost verbatim with this version. "What saith the Scripture?" says St. Paul, and immediately he proceeds to quote the Septuagint.

Scripture amongst all the "Jews of the Dispersion." What our Authorised Version is to the English-speaking races, that was the Septuagint to the ancient world. It was the "People's Bible," as far as such a name is applicable in speaking of those ancient days. It was written in the popular language. It was sold at the popular price, comparing with the Hebrew as our "Shilling Popular Editions" of books to-day compare with the elaborate guinea volumes. Consequently its influence was very important. It kept alive the knowledge of God when the "holy tongue" had fallen into disuse. It spread amongst the Gentiles the anticipation of the coming Messiah. It was the safeguard of Judaism amongst the scattered Israelites until Judaism had become a withered branch too dead and sapless to be worth safeguarding any longer, and then it became Christianity's chariot as it passed forth from its birthplace in Palestine to conquer the world. Humanly speaking, it is hard to see how Christianity could ever have succeeded without the Septuagint Bible.

Besides all this, it has a further claim on our attention here. It has much to do with Old Testament Biblical criticism as a most important witness of the Hebrew text, from which it was translated before Massoretic or even Talmud days.

Whence, then, came this Septuagint version? Who were its authors? Why was it made? What is its value in the investigation of the text?

No. 1.—A half-burnt fragment of the Codex Geneseos Cottonianus, a very valuable Septuagint Manuscript about 1400 years old.

No. 2.—Facsimile of its writing, full size.

No. 6.—Beginning of the 29th Psalm, from a papyrus manuscript of Septuagint in the British Museum.

(Photographed by kind permission of Professor Westwood, Oxford, from the Palæographia Sacra Pictoria.)

To face page 148.]

II.

The Romance of Aristeas.

There is a curious old letter extant professing to be written by Aristeas, a distinguished officer of Ptolemy Philadelphus, king of Egypt, in the third century B.C. It carries us back to the days of the famous Alexandrian Library, the literary treasure-house of the ancient world. It tells that the book-loving King Ptolemy, with the true passion of a collector, had set his heart on adding to his treasures a translation of the Hebrew Pentateuch, of which he had heard through his chief librarian, Demetrius Phalereus.

He was advised by Aristeas that it was no easy matter to procure it. " You certainly will not get it," said he, " while those thousands of Jewish slaves are suffering throughout your land." (I wonder if the King knew the story of his far-back predecessors and those other Jewish slaves which his new document would tell of.)

Ptolemy, however, was not to be baffled. He ordered an enormous sum of money to be expended, and 198,000 captives were immediately set free. Then was arranged a gorgeous procession to Jerusalem, of which this host of freed men formed the chief part—a second exodus of Israel from Egypt. With them they bore splendid presents to Eleazar, the high priest, fifty talents of gold, seventy talents of silver, besides tables and cisterns and bowls of gold

in lavish abundance; also a letter from the king,
requesting that there might be sent to him a copy of
the Law, and Jewish scholars capable of translating it.

Then comes the equally gorgeous account of the
return; of the seventy-two learned Hebrews, six from
each tribe; of the exquisitely fine·parchment manuscripts of the Law, "written in gold in the Jewish
letters;" of the royal reception prepared for them in
Alexandria; the seven days' feasting in the presence
of the king; the seventy questions testing their wisdom; and then the magnificent study prepared for them
by the sea, away from the bustle of the noisy streets,
where, in seventy-two days "of co-operation and confer-
ence," they gave to the world the Septuagint version !

Aristeas had surely not stinted in his wonders;
but in his day, as in our own, such stories seldom
lost in repetition. So we find in the early Christian
ages the additional touches that there were seventy-
two separate cells[1] (some say thirty-six) on the rocky
shores of the island of Pharos, in which the translators
worked independently of each other, and it was found
at the end that each had produced a translation
exactly word for word with all the others. Therefore,
of course, the work was miraculous—a direct inspiration of the Spirit of God !

When it was ended, Demetrius, the chief librarian,

---

[1] Justin Martyr, in the second century, tells us that he was shown
by his guide at Alexandria the ruins of these Septuagint cells ! If his
story does not prove the inspiration of the Septuagint, it proves, at any
rate, that, in the matter of the tales of tourist guides, there is nothing
new under the sun.

summoned the Jews of the city to the house where the translators had worked, and read the translation, which was heartily approved. Curses were pronounced on any who should dare to add to or take from it. The Jews received permission to take a copy. The king rejoiced greatly, and commanded the books to be carefully kept. He gave to each translator three robes and two talents of gold, with other gifts; to Eleazar, the high priest, he sent ten silver-footed tables and a cup of thirty talents, and begged that any of the translators who wished might come and see him again, for he delighted to meet such men, and to spend his wealth upon them.

III.

Who made the Septuagint?

This story, substantially repeated by Josephus, by the famous Philo the Jew, and by many of the Christian fathers, was generally received as the true account of the origin of the Septuagint until about two hundred years since. It probably explains the name "Septuagint," or "Seventy," applied to the version [1] (which is usually denoted by the numerals lxx.) from the number of the translators, and, doubtless, it also accounts in a great measure for the high repute in which this version so long was held.

---

[1] It is by some derived from the sanction given to the version by the Seventy of the Alexandrian Sanhedrim. It is held by others that the name Septuagint originally belonged to the Alexandrian Library, from the number of its founders, and was thence applied to this, one of its most famous documents.

It is now universally considered to be a mere piece of Eastern romance, invented to uphold the credit of the work. But it undoubtedly rests on a basis of fact. All the evidence points clearly to the facts, which are amply confirmed by the study of the work itself, that this Greek version originated in Alexandria in the time of the earlier Ptolemies, about 280 B.C., and that the nucleus of the work was certainly the Pentateuch. That the literary tastes of the Egyptian king had something to do with its origin may also be true, just as in New Testament days a Persian translation was ordered by the Emperor Akbar. But, clearly, the real cause of its existence must be sought in the needs of the scattered Jews of the Dispersion, who knew scarcely anything of Hebrew, and whose common language was the universal Greek.

One part of the story that must certainly, we fear, be put aside as pure fiction is that of the Palestine manuscripts and the scholars from Jerusalem coming to translate them. An examination of the work itself, with its imperfect knowledge of Hebrew, its mistakes about Palestine names of places, its Egyptian words and turns of expression, its Macedonic Greek which prevailed at Alexandria, and its free tendencies in translation, so opposed to the superstitious literalism of the Jewish schools, at once puts the Palestine origin of the version completely out of court. It was made by Jewish scholars of Alexandria, and not all of them very good scholars either, judging from their work. They show in many places a very imperfect knowledge of Hebrew, and indeed of Greek too, for that matter. They frequently mistake ordinary words for proper names, and sometimes try to translate proper names as if they were ordinary words. The similarity of the Hebrew letters is one of their great stumbling-blocks. We have already given examples of their errors from this cause as well as from their differences of Hebrew pronunciation. There are many mistakes, too, from the wrongly dividing or joining of words written probably without any division in the Hebrew manuscript before them; as, for example, in Ps. cvi. 7, *al yam*, " at the sea," which they translate, *alyam*, " going in."

IV.

Its Critical Value.

As to the value of the Septuagint in Textual Criticism, opinions are widely divided. Some scholars, pointing to the great antiquity of the translation, and to its frequent use by our Lord and the Apostles, would have us receive it as superior almost to the Massoretic Hebrew text. Others would entirely ignore its authority, telling us that its variations from the Hebrew arose " out of the carelessness and caprice of transcribers, their uncritical and wanton passion for emendation, and their defective knowledge of the Hebrew tongue " (Keil., Introd.). The truth lies between these extremes.

It is true that this Septuagint has been translated from a very ancient Hebrew Bible. It is true, too,

that in the time of the Septuagint translators some
variations existed in the Hebrew text.   There can be
little doubt either that in some places at least, where it
differs from the present Hebrew, the Septuagint preserves for us the truer reading.   But it would be very
dangerous to attempt many corrections on its sole
authority.   We have seen already what stupid mistakes it sometimes made, and there is much besides
to make us accept its evidence with great caution where
it differs from the Hebrew.

Tho several books were evidently translated by men
of very different attainments in scholarship, and without
any after revision to bring the various parts into har-
mony.   Then these Egyptian Jews were by no means
hampered with the rigid Palestine notions.   The fact
that they ventured to translate the Bible at all out of
the holy tongue, which would seem almost sacrilege to
the Jews of Tiberias ; their admission of the apocryphal
books into their Canon ; and still more, perhaps, the
existence of a schismatical temple in Egypt,[1] with its
priesthood and ritual, while they still recognised Jerusalem as the mother Church, all indicate a tone of
thought much freer and less scrupulous than that of
the Holy Land.   And accordingly we trace in their
translation a bold, free handling of the text before
them, often expanding and paraphrasing to bring out

---

[1] During the terrible Syrian persecution in Palestine, about 200 B.C.,
Onias, son of the murdered high priest, fled to Egypt.   King Ptolemy
received him kindly, and gave him a disused heathen temple at Leonto-
polis, which was converted into a Jewish sanctuary, with its Aaronic
priesthood and temple ritual.

the sense, or to gratify their love of diffuse writing. Evidently the meaning, not the strict letter of the text, was the chief consideration with them. True, the sense was, on the whole, fairly rendered. Indeed, were it otherwise we could not understand the use of the version by our Lord and His Apostles. But, at the same time, it is clear that this freeness, however useful, is a serious defect in an instrument of textual criticism when the object is to find out exactly what Hebrew words were in the manuscripts used by the translators.

But the chief difficulty in using the Septuagint is, that it is very difficult now to tell, with any certainty, what the Septuagint originally said. Even in the days of Origen, 1600 years ago, it had already grown so corrupt as to greatly need the revision of it which he attempted, and unfortunately his well-meant efforts only made matters worse. He compared it with the Hebrew Bibles of his day, supplying from the Hebrew what seemed to be omissions, and noting what seemed to him mistakes or additions. These additions and omissions, &c., he denoted by asterisks and crosses and other literary marks. But, as might be expected, in the course of frequent copying these marks of his got often misplaced, and often dropped out altogether, so that the cure in time became really worse than the disease.

Much has been done for it in recent years, but much still remains to be done, in the collecting of ancient copies and recording their various readings. As it

stands at present, the revisers cannot well be blamed
that they hesitated to use it more freely in their work,
though few would be inclined to go the length of their
American *confrères*, who practically advised that it
should be rejected altogether.

V.

Famous Septuagint Manuscripts.

The most ancient copies known of the Septuagint
are the Vatican Codex, an old manuscript of the
fourth century, preserved in the Vatican Library at
Rome, and the "Sinaitic," whose romantic story is
graphically told by Dr. Tischendorf, the finder of its
scattered sheets in the old paper basket at Mount
Sinai (see photograph on opposite page).

A little later in date is the Codex Alexandrinus, in
which we have a special interest, as it belongs to our
own nation, and may be seen any day in its case in
the British Museum." [1]   There is a small facsimile of
it in the plate facing p. 149, which exhibits also the
burnt fragment of another celebrated Septuagint copy,
the Codex Geneseos Cottonianus.

[1] For an account of these manuscripts see the writer's " How we got
our Bible " (Bagster & Sons).

One of the Oldest Manuscripts of the Septuagint. Photographed from one of the sheets found by Dr. Tischendorf in 1844 in an old fuel basket at Mount Sinai.

To face page 156.

I.

A witness to the Bible of the Scribes and Pharisees.

I place together in this bundle a set of old documents which are of considerable value in the textual criticism of the Old Testament. Chief amongst them are portions of three translations of the Hebrew Bible into Greek, made during the second century A.D. by three scholars, named Aquila, Symmachus, and Theodotion, and, therefore, witnessing to the Hebrew text that existed in the time of our Lord, and probably long before.

I dare not tax the reader's patience with any detailed account of these old Bibles. Let me, therefore, draw forth a single version from my bundle, and give it and its story as a specimen of the rest.

II.

Renegade and his Bible.

In the lovely city of Sinope, on the shores of the Black Sea, there lived in the second century a heathen gentleman named Aquila, a man of high position, connected by marriage with the imperial family of Rome.

One advantage of being connected with royalty was, in Aquila's day at least, the choice of a comfortable post in the Civil Service. By the Emperor's direction, he was commissioned to Jerusalem to examine and report on certain public buildings, and while residing there the amateur surveyor became converted to Christianity.

He was not, however, a very satisfactory convert. He still retained many of his heathen superstitions; and one day it was found necessary by the heads of the courageous little Church at Jerusalem that he should be publicly reprimanded. It was not the first time, nor will it be the last, that an honest rebuke has been the cause of a " 'vert " to some other religious body. Aquila, in anger, joined himself to the Jews; and having become circumcised, he soon began to pose as a most zealous defender of the Mosaic Law and ritual.

At this time a fierce controversy raged between Jews and Christians as to the interpretation of certain Messianic prophecies in the Old Testament; and as the Septuagint was the version chiefly appealed to by the latter it was sternly banned by the Rabbis as the " Christians' Bible." They even went so far as to compare the " accursed day when the seventy elders wrote the Law in Greek for the king " (Ptolemy) with that other day of evil in the ancient time " when Israel made for itself the golden calf."

It was necessary, of course, under these circumstances, that there should be a Greek translation other than the Septuagint for the use of the Jews who could not read the Hebrew, and their aristocratic convert, being a man of some scholarship, determined to undertake this task himself.

The Jews were delighted with the new work, and it gained so large a circulation that a new edition (that highest pleasure of an author) was called for within a few years of its first issue.

This is the specimen version, or rather the remains of it, that I have drawn out of my bundle of documents to exhibit. It follows the Hebrew with slavish literalness, so as, indeed, quite to spoil its own Greek. But this defect is its chief virtue for the purpose of textual criticism, as, of course, it makes it easier to find out the exact Hebrew words which the translator had before him. It would, therefore, be a most valuable help if we had it perfect; all the more so, since Aquila is said to have become a student of the great College of Tiberias, and on that account would be a witness to the very best Palestine text. Some interesting traces may be found in it of the controversial purpose with which it was prepared; for example, in Isa. vii. 14, " Behold a *virgin* shall conceive," &c., where he translates the word " young woman ; " not exactly a false translation, but yet evidently intended to turn the point of the Christians' argument.

Any notice of the other versions in the bundle would probably only tire the reader. From this account of Aquila's he will form some notion of the rest.[1] Therefore, it is only necessary, further, to say that the evidence of these versions goes to show that the Hebrew manuscripts from which they were translated in the second century corresponded very nearly with the Massoretic manuscripts in our hands to-day, though, at the same time, they exhibit some interesting variations which the Septuagint and other versions frequently support.

[1] St. Jerome tells us that Aquila sought to reproduce the Hebrew word for word ; that Symmachus aimed at a clear exposition of the sense ; while Theodotion's object was to make a revised edition of the Septuagint.

DOCUMENT No. V.

I.

St. Ephraem the Syrian.

Once upon a time, some fifteen hundred years ago, there lived a great father of the Syrian Church, generally known to scholars now by the name of St. Ephraem the Syrian. He was a very learned and thoughtful old writer, yet his name would probably have been as little remembered as that of many other learned and thoughtful writers of his day had it not been for its connection, partly accidental, with two great facts in the history of Biblical criticism.

The first was, that when the old man had been nearly a thousand years in his grave, some enthusiastic admirer one day wanted to copy out one of his lectures. But parchment for the purpose was expensive and difficult to be got. So, providing himself with a piece of pumice-stone, he or she—these enthusiastic admirers are generally ladies—coolly scrubbed out the writing of a very ancient and valuable copy of the Scriptures, for which there was probably little demand in that day, and wrote in its stead St. Ephraem's discourses. This old parchment was brought from the

L

East with a number of other manuscripts in the sixteenth century, and afterwards having passed into the possession of her family, was presented to the Royal Library at Paris by the infamous Catharine de Medicis.

In later days, when Biblical criticism had become an important branch of study, some dim traces of the ancient writing appearing underneath called the attention of scholars to the document, and by the repeated applications of chemicals the old obliterated Bible was at length partially restored, and the Paris Library thus became the possessor of one of the greatest literary treasures in the world, a Bible manuscript dating from the fifth century. From its accidental connection with the lectures of the old Syrian, this stained and blotted old Bible is now known as the " Codex of Ephraem." (See Plate, opposite.)

The other fact is, that Ephraem's greatest work was a commentary on the Syriac Bible of his day; and long ages afterwards, when the importance of the Syriac Bible became recognised in textual criticism and all the ancient Bibles such as Ephraem used had utterly disappeared, this commentary of his became, of course, a most valuable source of information about the old Syriac text.

II.

The Oldest Christian Bible.

This Syriac Bible is the most ancient of all the Christian versions. It was evidently growing anti-

SPECIMEN OF A "PALIMPSEST" MANUSCRIPT LIKE THAT OF ST. EPHRAEM.

(Notice under the writing the faintly appearing letters of the Old Bible
that had been rubbed out.)

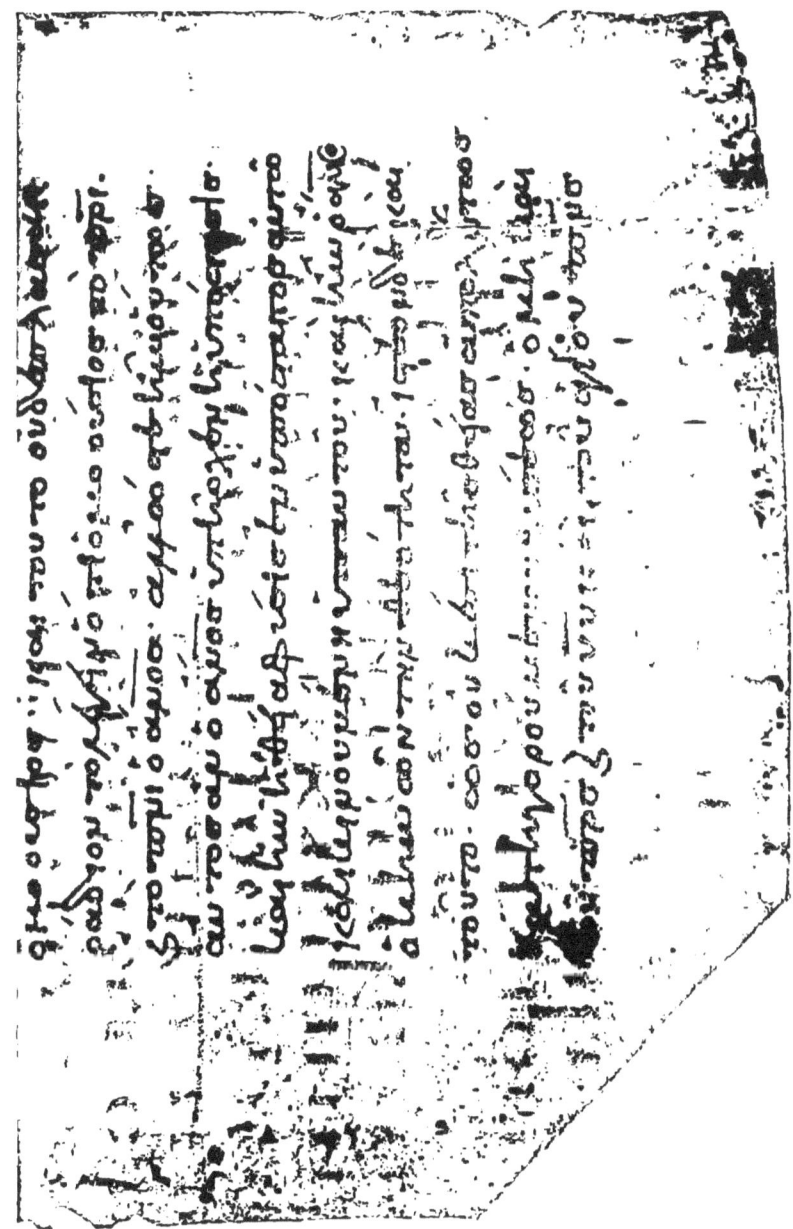

Photographed from the Dublin University Palimpsest, Codex Z

quated even in Ephraem's day (about A.D. 350), if we
may judge from his comments on the text. He
constantly finds it necessary to explain words and
phrases that had already become obscure to the people
of his time, though, by the way, he very often explains
them wrongly. The fact, however, that such explanations were needed is most probably an indication of
the antiquity of the Syriac text which lay before him.

Melito, bishop of Sardis, about the year 170, quotes
the reading of this Syriac Bible of a verse in Genesis;
and the great Origen, whom we have mentioned already,
and who lived about A.D. 250, tells of a Syriac Bible
manuscript in the possession of a poor widow whom he
knew. All the other evidence confirms the impression
thus left on us as to its date, and scholars are now
almost unanimous in placing the Syriac version not
later than about the year 150 A.D.

III.

Letter from the Lord Jesus to a Syrian King.

The traditions of the Syrian Church, however, are
by no means satisfied with so modern a date for their
Bible. One opinion puts the date of the Syriac Old
Testament back to the days of Solomon and Hiram,
when all the Hebrew books written up to that date
were, they say, translated into the Syriac tongue.
Another tradition tells that it was translated by the
priest, who was sent to Samaria by the Assyrian
king (2 Kings xvii. 28); while a third and some-

what more plausible statement is, that the version belongs to the days of Thaddeus the apostle and Abgarus, king of Edessa, the correspondent of our Lord.

Have you ever heard, reader, the ancient Church story of the evangelisation of Syria, the letter of King Abgarus written to Jesus Christ, and the answer of our Lord to that Syrian king? The story goes that, moved by the account of Christ's beautiful life, and of His unkind reception by the Jews, and needing also to be healed by Him of a sore disease, King Abgarus sent Him a letter inviting Him to his land, and generously offering to share with Him all that he had. The story was widely believed in the early centuries. It seems a pity we cannot believe it still. On reading the simple, touching letter, one is almost inclined to regret that we live in this clearer, colder age of historical doubt and criticism, in which all those beautiful old legends are withering away.

Here are the letters as given by Eusebius, the great Church historian in the fourth century. He says he found them in the archives of the library at Edessa, and translated them from their original Syriac tongue :—

Copy of the Letter written by King Abgarus to Jesus, and sent to Him at Jerusalem by Ananias the Courier.

ABGARUS, PRINCE OF EDESSA, SENDS GREETING TO JESUS, THE EXCELLENT SAVIOUR WHO HAS APPEARED ON THE BORDERS OF JERUSALEM. I HAVE HEARD THE REPORTS RESPECTING THEE, AND THY CURES AS PER-

FORMED BY THEE WITHOUT MEDICINE OR THE USE OF
HERBS. FOR IT IS SAID THOU MAKEST THE BLIND
TO SEE AGAIN, AND THE LAME TO WALK. AND THOU
CLEANSEST THE LEPERS, AND THOU CASTEST OUT IM-
PURE SPIRITS AND DEMONS, AND THOU HEALEST THOSE
THAT ARE TORMENTED BY LONG DISEASE, AND THOU
RAISEST THE DEAD; AND HEARING ALL THESE THINGS
OF THEE, I CONCLUDED IN MY MIND ONE OF TWO
THINGS; EITHER THOU ART GOD, AND HAVING DE-
SCENDED FROM HEAVEN, DOEST THESE THINGS; OR
ELSE, DOING THEM, THOU ART THE SON OF GOD.
THEREFORE, NOW I HAVE WRITTEN AND BESOUGHT
THEE TO VISIT ME, AND TO HEAL THE DISEASE WITH
WHICH I AM AFFLICTED.

I HAVE HEARD ALSO THAT THE JEWS MURMUR
AGAINST THEE, AND ARE PLOTTING TO INJURE THEE.
I HAVE, HOWEVER, A VERY SMALL BUT NOBLE ESTATE,
WHICH IS SUFFICIENT FOR US BOTH.

The Answer of Jesus to King Abgarus by the Courier Ananias.

BLESSED ART THOU, O ABGARUS, WHO, WITHOUT
SEEING, HAST BELIEVED IN ME. FOR IT IS WRITTEN
CONCERNING ME, THAT THEY WHO HAVE SEEN ME
WILL NOT BELIEVE; THAT THEY WHO HAVE NOT SEEN
MAY BELIEVE AND LIVE. BUT IN REGARD TO WHAT
THOU HAST WRITTEN, THAT I SHOULD COME TO THEE,
IT IS NECESSARY THAT I SHOULD FULFIL ALL THINGS
HERE FOR WHICH I HAVE BEEN SENT, AND AFTER THIS
FULFILMENT THUS TO BE RECEIVED AGAIN BY HIM
THAT SENT ME. AND AFTER I HAVE BEEN RECEIVED
UP, I WILL SEND TO THEE A CERTAIN ONE OF MY
DISCIPLES, THAT HE MAY HEAL THY AFFLICTION, AND
GIVE LIFE TO THEE AND THOSE WHO ARE WITH THEE.

After these letters, the historian gives the account,
which he found subjoined to them in the Syriac

tongue, of the fulfilment of our Lord's promise after
His Ascension, and the proclamation to Syria of the
Christian faith.   For many centuries it was believed
that Edessa had a charmed existence, being imper-
vious to all assaults of besiegers through its possession
of this divine epistle.

IV.

Biblical Criticism and the Syriac Bible.

At any rate, leaving these old traditions altogether
out of account, there is, as we have seen, clear proof
of the existence of this Syriac version soon after the
year 150.   It is, therefore, the earliest of all Christian versions.   St. Ephraem teaches us by the words
and phrases quoted in his commentary that the Syriac
text in our hands to-day is substantially the same as
that which he had before him.   We find the very
same words in our existing Syriac manuscripts.   And
we have further evidence of this from the fact that
soon after his day the Syrian Church split into three
hostile sects, hating each other as heartily as did the
Jews and Samaritans, but all three nevertheless using
to this day the same version of the Scriptures.   This
indicates clearly that the present Syriac Bible must
have been in use before the schisms in the Church,
since we cannot believe that after it any one of the
three hostile parties would have accepted its Bible
from another.

SPECIMEN OF SYRIAC.

PESHITO VERSION.

ܒܪܫܝܬ ܐܝܬܘܗܝ ܗܘܐ ܡܠܬܐ. ܘܗܘ ܡܠܬܐ
ܐܝܬܘܗܝ ܗܘܐ ܠܘܬ ܐܠܗܐ. ܘܐܠܗܐ ܐܝܬܘܗܝ
ܗܘܐ ܗܘ ܡܠܬܐ. ܗܢܐ ܐܝܬܘܗܝ ܗܘܐ ܒܪܫܝܬ
ܠܘܬ ܐܠܗܐ. ܟܠ ܒܐܝܕܗ ܗܘܐ. ܘܒܠܥܕܘܗܝ
ܐܦܠܐ ܚܕܐ ܗܘܬ ܡܕܡ ܕܗܘܐ. ܒܗ ܚܝܐ ܗܘܐ.
ܘܚܝܐ ܐܝܬܘܗܝ ܢܘܗܪܐ ܕܒܢܝܢܫܐ. ܘܗܘ
ܢܘܗܪܐ ܒܚܫܘܟܐ ܡܢܗܪ: ܘܚܫܘܟܐ ܠܐ ܐܕܪܟܗ ܀
ܗܘܐ ܓܒܪܐ ܕܐܫܬܕܪ ܡܢ ܐܠܗܐ: ܫܡܗ ܝܘܚܢܢ.
ܗܢܐ ܐܬܐ ܠܣܗܕܘܬܐ ܕܢܣܗܕ ܥܠ ܢܘܗܪܐ.
ܕܟܠܢܫ ܢܗܝܡܢ ܒܐܝܕܗ. ܠܐ ܗܘܐ ܗܘܐ
ܢܘܗܪܐ. ܐܠܐ ܕܢܣܗܕ ܥܠ ܢܘܗܪܐ. ܐܝܬܘܗܝ
ܗܘܐ ܓܝܪ ܢܘܗܪܐ ܕܫܪܪܐ: ܕܡܢܗܪ ܠܟܠܢܫ
ܕܐܬܐ ܠܥܠܡܐ. ܒܥܠܡܐ ܗܘܐ. ܘܥܠܡܐ
ܒܐܝܕܗ ܗܘܐ. ܘܥܠܡܐ ܠܐ ܝܕܥܗ. ܠܕܝܠܗ
ܐܬܐ. ܘܕܝܠܗ ܠܐ ܩܒܠܘܗܝ. ܐܝܠܝܢ ܕܝܢ
ܕܩܒܠܘܗܝ: ܝܗܒ ܠܗܘܢ ܫܘܠܛܢܐ ܕܒܢܝܐ
ܕܐܠܗܐ ܢܗܘܘܢ. ܠܐܝܠܝܢ ܕܡܗܝܡܢܝܢ ܒܫܡܗ.
ܐܝܠܝܢ ܕܠܐ ܡܢ ܕܡܐ. ܘܠܐ ܡܢ ܨܒܝܢܐ ܕܒܣܪܐ.
ܘܠܐ ܡܢ ܨܒܝܢܐ ܕܓܒܪܐ ܐܠܐ ܡܢ ܐܠܗܐ ܐܬܝܠܕܘ.
ܘܡܠܬܐ ܒܣܪܐ ܗܘܐ ܘܐܓܢ ܒܢ. ܘܚܙܝܢ
ܫܘܒܚܗ. ܫܘܒܚܐ ܐܝܟ ܕܝܚܝܕܝܐ ܕܡܢ ܐܒܐ:
ܕܡܠܐ ܛܝܒܘܬܐ ܘܩܘܫܬܐ ܀

[To face page 166.]

The great value of this Syriac version consists in
the fact that it is a translation *direct* from the Hebrew,
many of the other early versions being second hand,
made from the Septuagint translation. And its value
is increased owing to its excellence. It comes nearest
to our ideal of what a version ought to be. It re-
produces its original faithfully, and as far as possible
literally, seldom or never relaxing into free paraphrase.

Of course, the Hebrew manuscripts underlying it
are many centuries earlier than Massoretic days ; many
centuries earlier, it may be, even than the days of
our Lord.[1] It has several small variations from the
existing Hebrew Bible, sometimes evidently arising
from confusion of the " similar letters " or from reading the vowels differently from the Massoretes, but in
some cases exhibiting quite different and at times
apparently better readings than those of the Massoretic text.

Its chief defect for purposes of criticism is due to
traces of the influence of the Septuagint upon it. It
was almost inevitable that this should be so. The
Septuagint was the People's Bible, the Bible used by
our Lord and His Apostles, and circulated all over
the Christian Church. It would, therefore, be very
likely in process of time to tinge more or less all the
Eastern versions of the Old Testament.

[1] Christians have sometimes unfairly suspected that the Jews, in
their opposition to Christianity, may have tampered with the text of
Messianic prophecies. Therefore the importance of the Syriac Bible
is increased by the fact that it was made from a Hebrew Bible which
existed before any disputes between Jews and Christians.

The Syriac, like all the other ancient Bibles, still needs a great deal of revision before it can become a satisfactory instrument in the work of Biblical criticism. But there is ample store of material for the purpose. The Vatican and other great Continental libraries possess several important copies; and nearer hand, in the galleries of the British Museum is a richer collection than any, including the famous library treasures of the Monastery of St. Mary, Mother of God, from the Nitrian deserts in Egypt. So there is only wanting—and they are already coming forward—a band of earnest scholars to work at these old manuscripts, and give to the world a Syriac Bible worthy of its ancient history.

DOCUMENT No. VI.

THE "VULGATE" OF ST. JEROME.

I.

The Monk of Bethlehem.

Towards the end of the fourth century so many
variations had crept into the Old Latin Bibles that the
need of some kind of revision began to be very keenly
felt by every one who had the opportunity of comparing
two of them together. There were almost as many
different "editions," it was said, "as there were
copies."

Just at this crisis, when the leaders of the Latin-
speaking Churches were casting about for some one
to help them, there returned to Rome from his Bethlehem monastery one of the greatest Biblical scholars
of his day, Eusebius Hieronymus, better known to us
as St. Jerome, and his high reputation pointed him
out at once as the very man for this important work.
Jerome was not very willing at first to undertake it.
It is a thankless task, he said, and will only arouse
bitter prejudice amongst those "who think that ignorance and holiness are one and the same." However,
he was persuaded to attempt it, amid much advice
to be very tender of the prejudices of the "weak

brothers," whose consciences were so sensitive about meddling with the Scriptures, and he finished a rather cautious revision of the New Testament about the year 385. Then he began a Revised Version of the Psalms, correcting the current Psalters by means not of the original Hebrew, but of those Greek versions of Aquila, Symmachus, and Theodotion which we have just described. After this he went through a number of the Old Testament books, with a good deal of murmuring from his clerical friends that he was going too far with his changes in the Bible, and a good deal of dissatisfaction in his own mind that he was not going half as far as he ought to.

At last he grew tired of this cautious patching of old versions, which no amount of patching could mend, and so he determined on the bold stroke of going back to the fountain-head and translating the Old Testament direct from the original Hebrew manuscripts.

It was a very serious undertaking, and no other scholar in the Church of those days would have been competent to attempt it. But Jerome was a man of great resources. He was a most industrious and ener-getic worker, and an able and accomplished scholar. He was no novice in the task of translating; he had learned his Hebrew from the Palestine Rabbis; he had teachers from the College of Tiberias privately assisting him; he had access to Hebrew manuscripts probably centuries older than the time of our Lord. And, therefore, though he had many obstacles in his way; though his Hebrew scholarship was by no means

SCRAP OF AN "OLD LATIN" MANUSCRIPT, THE VERSION
WHOSE MISTAKES LED TO THE MAKING OF ST. JEROME'S
VULGATE (see p. 170).

*Photographed from Manuscript of Archbishop Ussher's, now in the Library
of Trinity College, Dublin.*

To face page 170.]

perfect; though there were no vowels in his Hebrew manuscripts to assist him in finding the meaning; though the fierce popular prejudice against changes considerably hampered the freedom of his work, he produced the most valuable translation of the Bible that has ever been made before modern days. No other work has had such an influence on the history of the Bible. For more than a thousand years it was the parent of every version of the Scriptures in Western Europe ; and even now, when the original Greek and Hebrew manuscripts are so easily accessible, the Rhemish and Douay Testaments are translations from this famous "Vulgate" Bible of St. Jerome, so are also our own Prayer Book Psalms, and the "Comfortable Words " in the Communion Office, while even in the Authorised Version of the Bible its influence is quite perceptible.

II.

The "Temper of a Saint."

Such a howl of indignation as this new Bible excited! Remembering the prejudice which our recent English Revised Bible excited a few years ago, it is instructive to recall the story how the work of the old monk of Bethlehem was received. It was called revolutionary and heretical; it was pronounced subversive of all faith in Holy Scripture ; it was an impious tampering with the inspired Word of God ; in fact, for centuries afterwards it was rejected and condemned, and everything was said that ignorant bigotry could suggest to bring it into disrepute. What a lesson on the evils of senseless prejudice! What an instance, too, of a brave, honest man determined to follow fearlessly what he felt to be right, even though the whole world were against him!

Even his greatest friends and admirers were swayed by the popular cry. St. Augustine, who was scholar enough to understand the merits of the work, and who had in the beginning praised and congratulated him, got frightened at the last. He begged him to let it alone. He told him the story of an old bishop in Africa, who used his (St. Jerome's) new-fangled translation; how one day, in reading the Lesson in Church, he read the word "ivy" instead of "gourd," in the story of Jonah, when the people started up in wild excitement, and refused to be quiet till they got their old Bible back.

Poor St. Jerome! it was a hard time for him, and his letters in existence tell how keenly he felt it. Unfortunately, too, whatever his other qualifications for the title, the old man had certainly not the "temper of a saint," and he slashed out bitterly against the "fools," the "stupids," the "two-legged donkeys" (bipedes asellos), whose prejudices had raised such an outcry against him. It is hard to blame him. It is a sad story to look back upon—a brave man wearing out his life in one of the grandest works ever accomplished for the Church, and seeing this

work of his by ignorant bigotry banned and pro-
scribed to his dying day!

It was long after his death before its value was
recognised. Pope Gregory the Great first set the
fashion by using it in his Commentary on the Book
of Job, and it is almost amusing to see how completely the tide had turned at the time of the Council
of Trent, when the injured old scholar had been a
thousand years dead. Men had then grown as
attached to the Vulgate of St. Jerome as those of
the fourth century had been to its predecessors. In
fact, they seem almost to have forgotten that it was
only a translation. When errors were pointed out,
they quite resented the idea of correcting it by means
of the old Greek and Hebrew manuscripts. "It is
the version of the Church," said they, "and in the
language of the Church. Why should it yield to
old Greek and Hebrew manuscripts which have been
in the hands of schismatics and unbelievers for hundreds of years?" So these wise scholars invented
an easy method of textual criticism for themselves.
Instead of going to the trouble of comparing the
version with the ancient manuscripts, they settled
the matter by calmly decreeing in Council that the
old Vulgate should be received as "authentic," whatever that may mean, and that it should be the standard version, to which appeal must be made in all
matters of controversy. An interesting exhibition of
the feeling at the time is a passage in the preface
to the great Complutensian Polyglot Bible, where the

Hebrew and the Greek and the Latin Vulgate were printed in parallel columns, side by side, the venerable old Vulgate being in the middle, which the editors, with grim humour, compared to the position of our Lord between the two thieves!

III.

Papal Infallibility and Biblical Criticism.

We have seen now that for centuries after St. Jerome the Vulgate had been banned and suspected; indeed, men had often presumed to "correct" it, so as to make it agree with the corrupt Old Latin Bible, which held the place of honour. The reader will therefore see reason to believe that by the time of the Council of Trent its copies had probably got into a state very much needing the exercise of intelligent textual criticism. The Council, as we have seen, contented themselves by declaring it "authentic," and decreeing that "hereafter the sacred Scripture, and especially this ancient Vulgate edition, should be printed as accurately as possible."

About forty years after, Pope Sixtus V. undertook to bring out a correct edition. His method was a very simple one indeed. He got together a company of learned revisers, but with this understanding, that their functions were merely to collect manuscripts and prepare the evidence for and against certain readings in the text, after which the Pope himself, by reason not of his scholarship, but of his gift of infallibility, decided straight off which were the genuine words! Then it occurred to him that it would be a good thing for the credit of his new edition if he forbade the collecting of any further critical materials, lest the authority of this sacred work should be undermined. He decreed also that all readings varying from his edition should be rejected as incorrect; that it should never be altered in the slightest degree, under pain of the anger of Almighty God and His blessed apostles Peter and Paul; and if any man presumed to transgress this mandate, he was to be placed under the ban of the major excommunication, not to be absolved except by the Pope himself!

But alas for "the best laid plans of mice and men"! Scholars who examined the new book very soon learned, if they did not know it before, that, as there was no royal road to learning, so was there also no papal road to criticism. The book was full of mistakes. The scholarship of Sixtus was by no means great, and his infallibility somehow failed to make up for this defect. The position was a very awkward one, and though things were kept quiet during the life of the Pope, as soon as he was dead it was strongly felt that his Vulgate would bring discredit and peril on the Church. At any cost, a new edition must be prepared to supersede the "infallible" one. But the credit of the deceased Pope must somehow be saved as well. How was this to be done?

I am afraid the Jesuits of that day do not come out of the matter with very clean hands. Only one way seemed open to them, and they adopted it. "The mistakes were all owing to the fault of the printer!" Not that they descended to a deliberate untruth. Dr. Salmon, in his recent book on "Infallibility," points out the delightful equivocation with which they salved their conscience. "Either the printers were to blame, *or somebody else,*" said they. But in the preface to the new edition brought out under Pope Clement VIII. the "somebody else" was left out altogether, and the whole blame of the Papal blunders was saddled on the unfortunate printer.

IV.

The Value of the Vulgate.

This new edition, the Clementine Vulgate, was a considerable improvement on its predecessor, but was very far from being a faultless work. Indeed, a satisfactory edition of the Vulgate now may almost be regarded as an impossibility. So many causes have united to corrupt it, that it is one of the hardest problems in textual criticism to restore the original "Bible of St. Jerome." But it is well worth doing all that can be done in this direction by means of the available ancient sources.

The document is a most important one. It is a witness of the Hebrew text at a very early period, for Jerome had probably manuscripts before him of an earlier date than the days of our Lord. And it must be remembered, too, that, like the Syriac, the Vulgate Old Testament is a translation *direct* from the Hebrew ;[1] not, like many other Christian versions, a second-hand translation from the Septuagint Greek. Therefore, it is worthy of much more pains than are being spent on it by Biblical scholars, and, even in its present faulty state, is a most valuable aid in the criticism of the Hebrew text.

[1] This is not true of the whole work. The Book of Psalms and a few of the apocryphal books were not translated from the original Hebrew, but were taken from the old Latin Bible, slightly revised by St. Jerome.

M

Book III.

THE NEW BIBLE.

A SPECIMEN OF

BIBLICAL CRITICISM.

CHAPTER I.

I.

Introductory.

"The Old Testament is sitting, sir!"

It called up rather absurdly reminiscences of the poultry-yard, this statement with which a pompous official barred the entrance to the Jerusalem Chamber to some visitors of our acquaintance during the recent revision days. The information really conveyed was that behind those closed doors the Biblical critics of the Revision Company were working at the materials accessible to them for producing a correct version of the Old Testament, and the visitors must retire without gratifying their curiosity about either the historic chamber or the work of the revisers.

I trust the reader's interest has been by this time sufficiently aroused to make him share their curiosity in the latter particular, for a glance at the work in the Jerusalem Chamber would be a most valuable illustration of our "Lesson in Biblical Criticism." We have already roughly examined the accessible material —the "Old Hebrew Documents" and the "Other Old Documents" described in the preceding pages. We have still to learn the method of using this material in producing a correct Bible, and the easiest way of doing so is by watching how it was used by the scholars of the Old Testament revision.

The reader will, of course, quite understand that this is not a book about the Revised or any other particular version. We merely desire to glance here at the recent revision, as the most convenient specimen accessible for our purpose. Let us therefore, in fancy, put aside the burly janitor from the doorway and view for a brief moment the "Old Testament sitting."

II.

"The Old Testament Sitting."

An ancient chamber, grand with historic memories, lined round with cedar and with curious tapestry—a long table running down the centre—a band of men busily intent on the written and printed sheets that lie spread out before them—a heavy face and monotonous voice arguing as to the value of a verse in the Septuagint which differs considerably from the Hebrew under discussion.

That is all. Nothing that seems very romantic or interesting about it. Does it differ from the scene which the reader expected? Is he looking round him for the beautiful gold and purple Psalters, or the rough, worn edges of old copies of the Law? Have I misled him, by the previous descriptions of the material, to imagine the floor piled with faded parchments from the archives of the East, and bishops and deans and reverend professors grubbing in the mouldering dirt of the old manuscripts, hurrying about from one document to another to investigate the evidence about the passages in question?

Comfort yourself, my reader. The parchments and the dirt are safe in their repositories all over the different libraries of Europe. The dirty work has been already done. For a hundred years past patient scholars have been toiling in many lands over the masses of ancient Biblical lore, and the results of their toil appear in the clean and carefully prepared sheets that lie on the revisers' table. Beside each column of the Hebrew are accurate annotations, telling of every important variation that has been discovered, whether in some of the Massoretic manuscripts, or in the Samaritan, or in certain copies of the Septuagint, or in the Syriac or Vulgate versions. If the Talmud or Targums, or any of the mediæval Jewish commentators, or any other authorities, have light to throw on a passage, their information too is carefully recorded. So that, it will be seen, the evidence for or against any particular reading is manifest at a glance.

III.

Defects of our Specimen.

Before proceeding to examine the work of the Old Testament revisers, it is necessary to remark that, though the most convenient specimen, it is by no means a good specimen for teaching how the various " Old Documents" ought to be used in producing a correct Bible. There are defects both in the material used and in the restrictions placed upon themselves by those who used them, which seriously hinder it from being a good illustration of the processes of Biblical criticism.

Partly perhaps from unwillingness to run counter to popular prejudices, but chiefly from difficulties connected with the state of the manuscripts, the revisers bound themselves to a close adherence to the Massoretic Hebrew Text. Now, however they might otherwise differ about their work, they all knew very well that this text was in many places of questionable integrity. Though, on the whole, it is safe to regard it as correct, though in the Pentateuch it reaches almost perfect accuracy, yet there were parts, especially the historical books, in which every scholar knew of superficial flaws and mistakes, some of which, too, were not very difficult of correction. But, except in rare cases, these flaws and mistakes had to be allowed to remain ; the revisers considered that, in the present state of our knowledge on the subject, it was best to adhere to the standard Massoretic text.

A good deal of blame has been attached to them for this "want of boldness" in accomplishing their work. It has been pointed out that the most ancient Massoretic manuscript is scarcely a thousand years old ; that the Septuagint and other ancient versions take us back much nearer to Old Testament

times; that they often give readings which quite
solve difficulties in the Hebrew text, and have every
appearance of being more correct; that sometimes it
is easy to prove from their translation that the mistake *must be* in the Hebrew, and to see exactly the
copyist's slip which gave rise to the mistake.

And all this is true. The Revised Old Testament
is decidedly behind the scholarship of the age. The
work is a timid and cautious one. There is little
doubt that the next revision, whenever it takes place,
will be bolder and freer, and that the ancient versions,
especially the Septuagint, will play a larger part in
the work. Yet, in spite of all this, we believe that the
revisers were fully justified in their cautious procedure.

For, in the first place, as we have seen already, there
is every reason to believe that the existing Hebrew
manuscripts, late though they be, differ but very
slightly from those in use at the time of our Lord,
and probably centuries earlier. The most important
of their flaws and defects are of very ancient times,
before any critical study of the manuscripts had
begun, and before any of the versions, except perhaps
the Septuagint, had been made.

And, in the second place, it must be remembered
that the versions, the only means of correcting the
Hebrew, are at present in a most unsatisfactory state.
The different copies of the Septuagint vary considerably from each other, and this too is the case with
the other old versions.

Therefore there is much to be said for the revisers'

explanation that the time is not yet ripe, that "our knowledge at present is not sufficient to justify an attempt at a reconstruction of the text by means of the Ancient Versions." The fact is, we were not ready for an Old Testament revision at all in this present century. The amount of necessary preparation work is simply enormous. We want a band of scholarly specialists to spend years in collecting and comparing the copies of the Septuagint, and by means of their critical wisdom to find out as nearly as possible what the old scholars of King Ptolemy really wrote down two thousand years ago. The same thing is needed for every one of the old versions, as far as it is possible to do it for them now. The Hebrew manuscripts themselves also need a good deal of careful study.

We must wait for all this to be accomplished. And we must wait, too—we shall not have long to wait—for the growth of a spirit of common sense in the public, whose prejudices have so much to do with rendering any new version a failure or a success. Our "Bible-loving people" must learn to aspire a little higher than the "rhythm" and "music" and "old associations," whose disturbance, I remember, was the chief burden of their criticism in the days of the late revision. They must get beyond this sentimental pietism, and see that, if necessary, all things else must be sacrificed to the one supreme object of making the Bible mean to us exactly what it meant to its original readers.

All these things will take time. On the whole, it may be safely asserted that for another half-century at least the time will not be ripe for a successful Old Testament revision.

IV.

Nineteenth Century Massoretes.

Under these circumstances, the revisers adopted a safe middle course. In cases of evident mistakes in the "Old Hebrew Documents," or of very plausible readings in the "Other Old Documents," they acted as did the old Massoretic revisers long ago—merely give the correction a place in the margin, only in very rare cases indeed making changes in the text. The reader will easily understand that the circumstances which necessitated this cautious procedure must considerably lessen the value of the Old Testament revision for our purpose as an illustration of Biblical criticism. For a good illustration it would be requisite that the "Hebrew Documents" should be freely open to correction, and that the "Other Old Documents," the instruments of that correction, should be in proper condition for accomplishing their task.

However, by carefully selecting our specimens for examination, we shall probably make it answer sufficiently for our purpose.

CHAPTER II.

SPECIMENS OF CRITICAL WORK.

I.

GEN. iv. 8 : And Cain talked with Abel his brother : and it came to pass, when they were in the field, that Cain rose up against Abel his brother, and slew him.

And Cain told Abel his brother : and it came to pass, &c.

MARGINAL READING.

Hebrew means, Cain said unto Abel his brother ; and many ancient authorities have, "said unto Abel his brother, Let us go into the field."

The Hebrew verb here means regularly said to, and when we meet it we always expect to find after it the words that were said. But there are no such words following it in the Hebrew text. Therefore, the translators of our Authorised Version saved the sense at the cost of the grammar, and incorrectly translated it talked with." The revisers have made a partial compromise—"Cain told Abel." The words literally translated would be :—

AND CAIN
SAID TO ABEL HIS BROTHER:
AND IT CAME TO PASS WHEN
THEY WERE IN THE FIELD THAT
CAIN ROSE UP, &C.

One is therefore inclined to suspect that the line containing the words which Cain said may have been lost out of the text by the slip of some copyist. They certainly do not occur in the "Old Hebrew Documents."

In this difficulty the revisers turned to the "Other Old Documents" to find out how they read the verse. First the Samaritan Pentateuch was called as a witness, and it read:—

AND CAIN

SAID TO ABEL HIS BROTHER,

LET US GO INTO THE FIELD.

AND IT CAME TO PASS, WHEN

THEY WERE IN THE FIELD, THAT

CAIN ROSE UP, &C.

This seemed a very likely reading. But then the Samaritan witness was not of too respectable a character. It had before been convicted of altering passages to make them read more smoothly and easily. Its evidence, therefore, could not be accepted without confirmation. Then they tried the Septuagint, which read just the same. The Syriac (Peshitto) was called, and then St. Jerome's old Vulgate, and last of all the two Jerusalem Targums, and they all persisted in inserting the words, "LET US GO INTO THE FIELD." There is a passage in 1 Sam. xx. 11 which also rather favours this insertion: "And Jonathan said unto David, Come, let us go into the field. And they went out both of them into the field."

It was argued in defence of the Hebrew reading, that the difficulty about the meaning of the verb might have made the other documents fill up the sense by inserting these words; while the Hebrew scribes were so scrupulous about the letter of the text that they would not meddle with it on any consideration. This may have been so, but the evidence seems very strong against it. I think, from the tone of the revisers' marginal note, that they were very much inclined to admit the disputed words into the text; and though now they must remain out in the cold for the present, their chances of admission are decidedly promising whenever the next Old Testament revision takes place.

II.

"AUTHORISED" READING.	REVISERS' READING.
GEN. xlix. 6 : In their self-will they digged down a wall.	In their self-will they houghed an ox.

It is hard to say which of these is the right reading. The Hebrew might mean either, according to the vowels supplied.

HQRU SHR might be read $\text{H}_a\text{QRU SH}_u\text{R}$, "they digged down a wall ;" or $\text{H}_i\text{Q}_o\text{RU SH}_o\text{R}$, "they houghed an ox." The Septuagint has the latter translation, and it seems to allude to the spirit of destructiveness manifested (compare 2 Sam. viii. 4); but most of the other versions have the reading of the "Authorised Version."

III.

" Authorised " Reading.	Revisers' Reading.
Josh. ix. 4: The Gibeonites went - and - made - as - if - they - had-been-ambassadors.	The Gibeonites took-them-provisions.

There is this improbability against the "Authorised" reading, that one does not quite see why the Gibeonites need *pretend* to be what they really were. That they "took them provisions," which is the reading in the Septuagint and of nearly all the ancient versions, fits in very well with their statement in verse 12 : "This bread which we took for provisions," &c.

The mistake, on whichever side it exists, is simply the confusion of our two mischievous old acquaintances, ד and ר, *d* and *r*. Here are the two words :—

(1.) הִצְטַיָרוּ = Hitztayaru = acted-as-ambassadors.
(2.) הִצְטַיָדוּ = Hitztayadu = took-them-provisions.

The first is the reading of nearly all the Massoretic manuscripts. Either the second was the word in the ancient Hebrew manuscripts which the Septuagint and other translators worked from, or else they mistook the other word for it. Who can tell which is right? The reader is now almost in as good a position to decide the question as were the revisers in the Jerusalem Chamber.

IV.

"Authorised" Reading.	Revisers' Reading.
Judges xviii. 30: And Jonathan, the son of Gershom, the son of Manasseh, he and his sons were priests (to the Danites' idol).	And Jonathan, the son of Gershom, the son of Moses, he and his sons were priests.

Here is a curious case of tampering with the Hebrew
text such as the Massoretes would never have dared to
attempt. It was done a thousand years before their
day. The Hebrew Bible, following the best manuscripts, has the word written thus, M^{N}SH, the N being
what is called "suspended." The name, therefore, is read
as MNSH (MANASSEH); though, if the little suspended
N were removed, it would be MSH = Mosheh (MOSES).
Clearly "MOSES" is the true reading, for Gershom
was the son of Moses, not of Manasseh, and Jonathan
is expressly stated to be a Levite, not a Manassite.

So far the evidence of the "Old Hebrew Documents."
Now let us see what the "Other Old Documents"
have to say. The reading "MANASSEH" appears in
the Septuagint, and therefore must have been in the
Hebrew manuscripts used by the famous "Seventy
Translators." It is found also in the Syriac, and
indeed in all the important versions with the exception of the Vulgate. St. Jerome's old Rabbis must
have taught him that it was wrong. It is clearly a
reading of very ancient times. But in spite of all
its supporters and all its antiquity, the reader will
easily see that it needs to be corrected.

There was probably not the least intention amongst the Jews of falsifying the text in this place. They scrupulously kept the נ small and suspended, and had a note in the margin calling attention to it. It was only that they hated to hear the name of Moses read in such a connection, and so, to spare their feelings, they pronounced it as Manasseh.[1] The Talmud has a note accounting for the reading :—" Gershom is called the son of Manasseh. Was he not the son of Moses? For it is written, The sons of Moses were Gershom and Eliezer. But because he did the works of Manasseh the idolater, the Scripture hangs him on to the family of Manasseh." And Rashi, the Jewish commentator mentioned already, tells us, " For the honour of Moses נ was written, but it was suspended to indicate that it was not Manasseh, but Moses."

V.

"AUTHORISED" READING.	REVISERS' MARGIN.
I SAM. xiii. 1 : Saul reigned one year, and when he had reigned two years over Israel.	Saul was (thirty) years old when he began to reign, and he reigned two years over Israel.

Beyond all question the Hebrew Bible is here corrupt. The usual formula for stating a king's age at his accession and his length of reign is :—" ———— was ———— *years old when he began to reign, and he*

---

[1] With the same object they substituted *bosheth* for *Baal* in proper names, Ishbosheth for Eshbaal, Mephibosheth for Meribaal, Jerubesheth for Jerubaal, &c., to avoid pronouncing the accursed name.

N

reigned ——— years." For example, 2 Sam. ii. 10 :
" Ishbosheth *was* forty *years old when he began to reign,
and he reigned* two *years.*"   2 Sam. v. 4 : " David *was*
thirty *years old when he began to reign, and he reigned*
forty *years* ; " and so frequently in the Books of Kings.
Now, this is the formula used above, and it cannot be
rightly rendered, as in our Bibles, " Saul reigned one
year ; " it should read, according to the Hebrew,
" Saul was one year old," which is clearly a mistake.
Probably the scribe, in writing the formula, left the
numerals blank, to be afterwards filled in, and thus the
mistake arose. The Septuagint does not help us much.
Some of its later editions have the word *thirty,* as
above, but the best MSS. leave out the verse.

It is very likely that in the ancient and less
scrupulous days some scribe thought this a convenient place for inserting in his manuscript the
usual information about the king's age and reign.
All we can say now is, that this verse is corrupt, and
we cannot tell what the true reading should be.

VI.

" AUTHORISED " READING.	REVISERS' MARGIN.
1 SAM. xiv. 18 : And Saul said unto Ahiah, Bring hither the ARK of God. For the ark of God was at that time with the children of Israel.	The Septuagint has— Bring hither the EPHOD ; for he wore the ephod at that time before Israel.

The Septuagint here is very probably right, though
the revisers have left the text uncorrected.   Let the

reader judge for himself. Here are the chief considerations that influenced them in admitting into their margin the Septuagint reading :—

(1.) The ark was, most probably, not there at all at the time, but at Kirjath-jearim (1 Sam. vii. 1, 2), where it remained from its capture by the Philistines until David removed it.

(2.) The ark would have been of no use for Saul's purpose. He wanted to ascertain the Divine will, and it was the ephod, not the ark, that was the instrument for doing so.

(3.) The words, " Bring hither the ark," are never used. The Hebrew verb here is suitable only to the bringing of smaller objects. Bring hither the ephod is a usual expression (see chap. xxiii. 9 ; xxx. 7).

(4.) Moreover, the words, *withdraw thine hand, i.e.,* desist, would not be appropriate if he were ordering Ahiah to get ready the ark to be carried out to battle.

(5.) The mistake of ark for ephod might easily take place. Here are the words—

ארון = Ark.

אפוד = Ephod.

Besides, too, it was noticed that, though the present authorised reading seems so smooth in English, in the original Hebrew it is defective and ungrammatical. Thus, "The ark was that day and (*not* with) the children of Israel."

On the whole, I think the reader will see that it is extremely probable, to say the least, that the Septuagint preserves for us the correct reading which was in the very ancient Hebrew manuscripts, and that our Massoretic manuscripts in this instance are corrupt.

VII.

The Story of David and Goliath (1 Sam. xvii., xviii.).

The revisers have rightly noted in the margin of 1 Sam. xvii. 12 that the episodes immediately before and after the combat with the giant (*i.e.*, vers. 12–31 and ver. 55, &c.) are omitted in the Septuagint. It was objected by some that this note was not justified, because that the famous Alexandrian manuscript of the Septuagint does not omit these parts. This is quite true, but on examining that manuscript it is found to be almost a stronger proof than if it had made the omission. Clearly the scribe who wrote it was accustomed to a manuscript which omitted these disputed parts. For immediately after finishing ver. 11 he begins the first words of ver. 32, as if they were the words immediately following, and then suddenly stops and proceeds to incorporate the missing section. But he does not score out the words of ver. 32 which he had begun, and so the traces of his correcting himself remain clear in the manuscript for 1500 years. Most probably he remembered just then, or somebody pointed out to him, that the Hebrew manuscripts contained this other section, and so he decided that it ought to be in the text in that place.

Ought it? How well I remember as a boy the difficulties which this story presented to me as it stands in our English Bible! Has it not often seemed strange to you, reader? Just before, we are told how David was introduced to the court of Saul, and became a prime favourite with the king, and was made his armour-bearer. Yet here he is represented as back amongst the sheep-folds, sent by his father to his brethren, treated by these brethren with a sharpness such as kings' favourites are certainly not often subjected to. Nay, we find that he is altogether unknown at court. The king has to inquire of Abner, who is unable to answer him, "Whose son is this youth?"

All this is very puzzling. Strike out the passages omitted by the Septuagint and all follows smoothly. Ver. 32 follows quite naturally after ver. 11, and xviii. 6 after xvii. 54. The story is then perfectly consistent. Nay, more. The Hebrew text shows some traces of having been pieced together at ver. 12, and it will be seen, too, that the omitted passages when put together form in themselves a complete story. It looks very like, indeed, as if the Septuagint were right, and that these passages had become inserted in the Hebrew text out of some other written account of the story, or else that they have got out of their proper place in the book.

And yet it may well be retorted, as it often has been, that the Septuagint translators, not feeling their responsibility about the text as the Palestine Jews did, were not at all above striking out passages which presented difficulties to their minds. It may be so. Certainly if it were in the Pentateuch it was asserted that this serious interpolation had occurred we should be very slow to believe it except on the most indisputable evidence. But in the early ages the manuscript of the Book of Samuel, which was used more for private circulation, and never regarded with the same high degree of reverence as were the Books of Moses, might quite possibly have had this disputed part inserted between its leaves by some private owner, and thus become the source of an error such as this.

At any rate, in the present state of the evidence the revisers would not be justified in altering the text.

VIII.

2 SAM. xxi. 19: And Elhanan, the son of Jaare-Oregim, a Beth-lemite, slew Goliath the Gittite, the staff of whose spear was like a weaver's beam.

Poor Goliath the Gittite! Surely we all thought that, if we knew anything of Hebrew history, we knew even from nursery days that he had been pretty well killed already by David himself, when he drew the giant's sword "and slew him, and cut off his head therewith."

Of course, we at once suspect some corruption. But how are we to hunt it down? Fortunately there is a parallel history, 1 Chron. xx., evidently copied from the same source, and corresponding word for word, except that it tells that Elhanan, the son of Jaar, "slew *Lahmi, the brother of Goliath.*" How are these two statements to be accounted for ?—

JAAR THE BETHLEMITE SLEW GOLIATH.
JAAR SLEW LAHMI, THE BROTHER OF GOLIATH.

At the sound of the word L_aHMI the Hebrew scholar at once pricks up his ears. He knows that this word, being in what we should call the objective or accusative case, will have in Hebrew the sign of that case, the particle ETH, before it; thus ETH-LHMI. Immediately he jumps to the conclusion that the word BTHLHMI (the Bethlemite), in the other passage, is a mistake for ETHLHMI. Thus set on the track, he sees how easily the word "brother" might have become lost or confused in the text.

ETH-GOLIATH   is   את-GOLIATH.
Brother of GOLIATH is   אחי-GOLIATH.

If the lines be placed directly under each other, the reader will see at once how easily a copyist might make the mistake :—

ETHLHMI אחי-GOLIATH = (slew) ETH-L$_a$HMI, BROTHER OF GOLIATH.
BTHLHMI את-GOLIATH = BETHLEMITE (slew) GOLIATH.

IX.

"Authorised" Reading.	Revisers' Reading.
2 Sam. xv. 28 : I will tarry in the **plain** of the wilderness.	I will **tarry** at the **fords** of the wilderness.

The reader will remember what has been said (p. 97) about the Massoretic marginal notes, the Keri and Kethibh. This is an illustration. The text has "Habaroth" (fords), the Keri (note in the margin) says, "read Haraboth" (plains). It also interestingly exhibits a very common form of transcriber's mistake. The writer, raising his eyes to the copy before him, repeats to himself the word "Haraboth," and then, before he has half-written it, it gets confused in his mind with Habaroth, which is so very like it in sound and appearance.

It is very hard to say which is right. The Kethibh, "fords," looks the most suitable to the context (see chap. xvii. 16); yet all the ancient versions support the Keri.

X.

"Authorised" Reading.	Revisers' Reading.
2 Sam. xviii. 13 : Wrought false-hood against **mine own** life.	Dealt falsely against **his** life.

Here is another of the Keri notes. The text has Naphsho (his life), but the Massoretic note in the margin says, "Read Naphshi" (my life). As already pointed out, we cannot place much dependence on these notes of the Massorah scribes. We have to use our judgment and the ancient versions in deciding between the reading of the text and the margin. Here the evidence of the versions is too conflicting to help us.

XI.

"AUTHORISED" READING.	REVISERS' MARGIN.
1 KINGS xiii. 12, 13: The father said unto them, Which way went he? Now, his sons had seen which way the man of God went. And he said unto his sons, Saddle me the ass.	The father said unto them, Which way went he? And his sons shewed him which way the man of God went. And he said unto his sons, Saddle me the ass.

Now, reader, which of these two readings seems to you the more probable? Is it not beyond question the second? The father asks which way, the sons shew him, and immediately he commands, " Saddle me the ass."

But, as has been already pointed out, it is a dangerous thing to decide by our notions of probability. Let us see what other considerations besides decided the revisers.

Hebrew verbs have what we may call a causative voice. Thus here the verb *to see*, when in this causative voice, would mean *to cause to see*, i.e., *to shew*. To see and to shew, then, are parts of the same verb, and are to be distinguished only by a slight difference in the vowels. Therefore, a confusion might easily arise between—

Y₁RU = his sons *had seen*.
YₐRU = his sons *shewed him*.

So when this alternative reading was proposed at the revision, the first inquiry was, What does the old Septuagint say? And on examination it was found that it read "*they shewed*," indicating that that was how the translators read this (vowelless) word in the ancient Hebrew manuscripts used in the making of it.

This, together with the plausibleness of the reading, was a strong point in its favour. Next the Vulgate was questioned, then the Syriac, and finally the Targums, and all persisted in reading with the Septuagint, "his sons *shewed him*."

It was argued, however, on the contrary side, that the Vulgate and Syriac, though translations direct from the ancient Hebrew, might have been influenced in the course of centuries by the all-powerful Septuagint, and therefore, perhaps, should not count as additional witnesses. In any case, it was said, the Hebrew gives a good and fairly probable sense, which, without greater reason, ought not to be disturbed.

Finally the question came to the vote, and since a majority of two-thirds was requisite for any change in the text, the new reading had to content itself with a place in the margin.

XII.

"Authorised" Reading.	Revisers' Reading.
1 Chron. vi. 2S : And the sons of Samuel ; the first-born **Vashni**, and Abiah.	And the sons of Samuel ; the first-born (**Joel**), and the second Abiah.

This correction was certainly needed, and it is a curious instance of how mistakes arise.

We learn from 1 Sam. viii. 2 that the first-born of Samuel was Joel, and the second Abiah ; and the 33rd verse of this chapter speaks also of Joel, the son of Samuel. Therefore the name Vashni, as the first-born, in the above verse, has always been rather a puzzle, and the only explanation was that offered in the margin of our Authorised Version, that Vashni must have been another name for Joel. To the English reader this may seem a fairly plausible explanation ; but let him take this short Hebrew lesson before making up his mind :—

  V is the Hebrew conjunction " and."
  SHNI means " the second."
  Therefore VSHNI = " and the second."

Now, the Hebrew manuscripts read thus :—

| AND THE SONS OF SAMUEL THE FIRSTBORN VSHNI ABIAH. | *i.e.,* AND THE SONS OF SAMUEL . . . THE FIRSTBORN, AND THE SECOND ABIAH. |

After reading the name Joel in the other passages as the first-born, does it not at once occur to the reader to suspect that the word JOEL has by some accidental slip of a copyist dropped out of the text, and that the copyist consequently, puzzled by the Hebrew word VSHNI ("and the second"), where no first had been mentioned, has vocalised it as a proper name, V_aSHNI, as though it were the name of Samuel's first-born ? Supply the word JOEL in the blank space above, and the whole difficulty disappears.

This is one of those extremely rare cases where we
seem compelled to go against all the Old Documents.
The blunder is more than two thousand years old.   It
was even in the ancient Hebrew manuscripts from which
the Septuagint translators worked two thousand years
ago, and they, of course, transferred it to their version,
where it exists to this day.   The Syriac is the only
important version which corrects it.

XIII.

Ps. xxii. 16 : *They pierced* my hands and my feet.

Here is a very remarkable case where the Hebrew
text has been entirely deserted in our English Bibles
for the preferable reading of the versions.

We saw in Bk. i. p. 16 how mistakes might
arise from the confusion of the two similar letters
י and ו (*y* and *u*).   Here is a case in point.   The
Hebrew in this famous passage makes no sense as
it stands.   The word translated " *they pierced* " is not
even a verb at all.   It is a noun, ARI (אֲרִי), " a lion,"
with a preposition K' (כּ) prefixed, so that it reads
K₄ARI (כַּאֲרִי), " like a lion."

" Like a lion my hands and my feet " is clearly.
sheer nonsense.   But if the little י at the end be
lengthened to ו, it becomes the Hebrew verb K₄ARU
(כָּארוּ), " they pierced."   Therefore, of course, there
can be no doubt that this is the right reading, and

that a mistake has arisen owing to confusion of two similar letters.

However, to make assurance doubly sure the Ancient Versions were consulted. The Septuagint reads, " They pierced ; " the Syriac and the Vulgate read the same ; and the other versions all practically confirm it, though some of them read a slightly different word.

This being one of the prominent Messianic texts, the charge of wilfully corrupting it was brought against the Jews, and largely believed, too, in those days, when anything evil was but too readily believed of them. But the charge is utterly unfounded. Though they kept this form of the word in the text, they always *read* it " they pierced," and it would seem that their reason for not correcting it even in the margin was because they held that the form K_aARI was grammatically consistent with the correct reading. The word occurs only once more in the Bible, Isa. xxxviii. 13, " *Like a lion, so will He break all my bones,*" and there is an interesting note in the Massorah stating that it occurs only in these two places, and that it has a different signification in each, thus clearly showing that in this verse of the Psalms they did not read it " like a lion.". The fact, too, that all the versions read it as a verb, even those of Aquila and Symmachus, who were so deeply imbued with the teaching of the Palestine Jews, points to the same conclusion.

XIV.

"AUTHORISED" READING.	REVISERS' READING.
ISA. ix. 3 : Thou hast multi-plied the nation, and **not increased** the joy ; **they joy before Thee** according to the joy in harvest, &c.	Thou hast multiplied the nation ; Thou hast **increased to it** the joy ;[1] they joy before Thee, &c.

The new reading is so much more in keeping with the whole jubilant tone of this Lesson for Christmas Day, that it will commend itself to many who know nothing at all about the reasons for changing it. The "not increased their joy" always sounded so like a discord in the Christmas music. Yet, when we examine the Hebrew manuscripts, we find that all, except about ten or eleven, contain the objectionable reading. What right, then, had the revisers to change it ?

There are two little Hebrew words of similar sound, rather like each other, too, in appearance, but very different in meaning. They are—

$$\text{לֹא} = \text{LO} = \text{not},$$
$$\text{לוֹ} = \text{L'O} = \text{to it};$$

and the question is which of these ought to be in the text. If the first be right, we must read, "NOT increased the joy;" if the other, "increased TO IT the joy."

Now, though the first is in the text of the manu-

---

[1] Freely translated, "Thou hast increased their joy," Revised Version.

scripts, there is an asterisk placed over it by the Massoretic scribes, indicating what seemed to them an error, and directing us to a footnote, which says, " Keri l'o," that is, "l'o should be read." True, we have sometimes to reject these Massoretic corrections as erroneous ; but here the context seems so obviously to require this reading, that the revisers felt themselves compelled to accept it, more especially when, on examining the Targum and the Syriac and other ancient versions, they found them, for the most part, in agreement with it.

In Ps. c. 3 is a similar correction, and on the same grounds, "It is He that hath made us, and NOT we ourselves," reads in the Revised Version, "It is He that hath made us, and we are HIS." Here, however, the old reading seems just as likely to be right as the new one.

CHAPTER III.

I WANT here to illustrate very briefly a further use of the " Other Old Documents" in producing a correct Bible. Where a word occurs only once or twice in the Hebrew Bible, or where, from any other cause, its meaning is doubtful, these Old Versions are very useful in settling its correct translation. True, we cannot always entirely depend on them. One of them will sometimes contradict another. But it is evident that it must be a considerable help in deciding the meaning if we know how men two thousand years ago understood the word. Here are a few specimens and illustrations :—

I.

"AUTHORISED" READING.	REVISERS' READING.
GEN. xii. 6: Abram passed through the land . . . unto the **plain** of Moreh.	Unto the **oak** of Moreh.

The meaning of the Hebrew word is doubtful. St. Jerome had to translate it in making his Vulgate 1500 years ago, and he rendered it *the plain*, and so do also the chief Jewish authorities. But the old Septuagint, 600 years earlier, always translates the word *oak*, showing that that was the meaning it conveyed to them; and the Syriac gives the same rendering.

II.

"AUTHORISED" READING.	REVISERS' READING.
GEN. xxx. 11 : Leah said, A troop! and she called his name Gad.	Leah said Fortunate! and she called his name Gad.

The word cried out by Leah was GAD! It might possibly mean a troop, but it is not easy to fix its derivation. In our difficulty we turn to the Ancient Versions. The Septuagint has, "In good fortune!" The Vulgate has, "Fortunately!" The Syriac reads, "My fortune cometh!" The Targum of Onkelos, "Fortune cometh!" the Targum of Jonathan, "My good star cometh!" so that evidently the whole weight of ancient testimony favours the new interpretation.

III.

"AUTHORISED" READING.	REVISERS' READING.
Ex. xxxiv. 13 : Ye shall destroy their altars, break their images, and cut down their groves.	And cut down their Asherim.
	MARGIN.
	Probably the wooden symbols of the goddess Asherah.

Here is a case where the English versions sought in the Ancient Versions the meaning of a word, and were set wrong by them. The Hebrew word is

O

ASHERIM, and the old English translators could not tell
what the strange word meant to its original readers;
but they found that St. Jerome's Vulgate translated
it "groves." St. Jerome had probably gone to the
Septuagint for the meaning, for we find it thus rendered by the old scholars of King Ptolemy. Evidently
they were as much puzzled by the word as was St.
Jerome, or the English translators who followed
his lead. Thus the word " groves " got into the
English Bible, and thus it remains to the present
day.

But any one who will carefully examine the different
passages where it occurs will see at once that it cannot
mean "groves." To "make," "set up," "break," are
not terms generally used of a grove of trees. It most
probably denoted some movable object of worship;
perhaps a figure of the goddess Ashtoreth, or, at any
rate, some rude wooden image used in connection with
heathen worship. See, for example, 2 Kings xxiii. 6,
where Josiah brought out the *grove* from the house of
the Lord, and burnt it, and stamped it to powder;
2 Chron. xvii. 6: Jehoshaphat took away the groves,
&c., &c. The revisers, in their difficulty, cut the knot
by simply printing the Hebrew word in English letters,
and letting the reader make what he could of it; so
now the time-honoured " groves " are in future to be
known as the " Asherim."

IV.

"AUTHORISED" READING.   REVISERS' READING.
LEV. xvi. 8, 10, 26 :   The other lot for AZAZEL.
The other lot for the scapegoat.

This is the only place where the Hebrew word
AZAZEL occurs in the Old Testament, and the question
of its meaning is a long-standing difficulty. The
English versions, from the " Great Bible " down, have
taken the interpretation from St. Jerome's Vulgate.
He renders it " *caper emissarius*"—" the goat that was
sent out." Probably this was a guess from the context, or perhaps he got it from the old Bible of
Symmachus (see Book ii. p. 158), who gives a similar
meaning. The Septuagint translates it vaguely, as if
at a loss what to make of it. Some other early writers
think it means the devil. The Jews of the Middle
Ages tell us that it meant some evil spirit. Where
all was so hazy, doubtless the revisers acted wisely in
leaving it as they found it, simply, as in the previous
case of the Asherim, expressing the Hebrew pronunciation in English letters, and so not committing themselves to any theory on the subject.

V.

"AUTHORISED" READING.   REVISERS' READING.
JUDGES viii. 13 : Gideon re- Gideon returned from the battle
turned from the battle **before the** **from the ascent of Heres.**
sun was up.

The word HERES *does* mean the sun, but it may also

be a proper name; see i. 35, ii. 9. What is the true meaning? Did Gideon return "before the rising of the sun," or "from the height of Heres?" The Vulgate says the former, and most Jewish commentators agree with it. The Septuagint says "from the ascent of Ares." Where doctors differ who shall decide?

VI.

"AUTHORISED" READING.	REVISERS' READING.
2 SAM. viii. 18: David's sons were **chief rulers**.	David's sons were **priests**.

This is a very startling translation, if it be correct. If David's sons were priests, there must have been a serious neglect of the law which restricted the priesthood to the family of Levi. The Hebrew word used is the same that in v. 17 is applied to Zadok and Ahimelech the priests. It is also used of Ira the Jairite in ch. xx. 26, and later, in the list of Solomon's officers, of Zabud the son of Nathan, who was "a KOHEN, and the king's friend." But surely it is possible that it may mean a chief minister either of Church or State. The Vulgate renders the word "priests," and is followed by Luther and by Coverdale's Bible; but the Septuagint has "courtiers," and both the Syriac Bible and the Targums have "princes." So, as far as the guidance of the Old Versions will take us in fixing the translation, we cannot go along with the recent revisers. The question, however, is a very difficult one, and important issues concerning what is called the higher criticism (see footnote, p. 37) are affected by it.

VII.

"AUTHORISED" READING.	REVISERS' READING.
I KINGS xxii. 38: And one washed the chariot in the pool of Samaria, and the dogs licked up his blood, and they **washed his armour.**	And they washed the chariot by the pool of Samaria, and the dogs licked up his blood: now **the harlots washed themselves** there.

The Hebrew word whose meaning is in question is ZONOTH. Now, in Hebrew, of course, as in English, it may happen that entirely different meanings may grow on to the same word.[1] The Hebrew word ZONOTH has not only the signification *armour*, but also, and much more frequently, the very different meaning, *harlots*.

Which does it mean in the passage before us? It is possible, to be sure, that the writer meant to inform us of the washing of Ahab's blood-stained armour. But considering the commoner signification of the word, does it not seem more probable that he meant to give an additional touch of ignominy to Ahab's wretched fate, by telling us that it was the pool where the harlots washed themselves in which the blood of the dead king was washed from the chariot?

We turn to the Ancient Versions to aid us in the inquiry, and find that the Syriac Bible eighteen cen-

[1] Take, for example, the English word *post.*

turies ago rendered the word "armour." The Targum gives the same signification. But the old Septuagint translators, four hundred years earlier, give it its commoner Hebrew meaning, "The harlots washed themselves;" and we see the revisers have thought fit to follow their lead.

I have nothing to do with the question as to which is the better translation, as my object is but to illustrate this use of the Ancient Versions.

And now, reader, our "Lesson in Biblical Criticism" is over. We have inquired into the accuracy of the Hebrew Writings, we have made the acquaintance of the chief Ancient Bibles of the world, we have learned some rudiments of Biblical Criticism, and, like schoolboys, worked out for ourselves little problems in our newly-acquired science. I trust all this may have been worth the doing, and may result in a more intelligent interest in the Bible. If the "Lesson" bring half as much interest and instruction to its learner as the preparation for it has brought to the teacher, it certainly will not have been learned in vain.

INDEX.

THE END.

www.ingramcontent.com/pod-product-compliance
Lightning Source LLC
Chambersburg PA
CBHW020057030726
47498CB00006B/1829